# In the Cold
# of the Malecón
## & Other Stories

# In the Cold
# of the Malecón
# & Other Stories

## Antonio José Ponte

Translated from the Spanish by
Cola Franzen and Dick Cluster

City Lights Books
San Francisco

Copyright © 2000 by Antonio José Ponte
Translation copyright ©2000 by Cola Franzen and Dick Cluster
All Rights Reserved
10 9 8 7 6 5 4 3 2 1

Cover design: Rex Ray
Cover photograph © Rick Gerharter
Book design: Small World Productions, San Francisco

Library of Congress Cataloging-in-Publication Data

Ponte, Antonio José, 1964–
    In the Cold of the Malecón and other stories / by Antonio José
    Ponte; translated by Cola Franzen and Dick Cluster.
        p.cm.
ISBN 0-87286-374-3 (pbk.)
1. Ponte, Antonio José, 1964– —Translations into English.
I. Franzen, Cola. II Cluster, Dick 1947– III.Title.
    PQ7390.P59 P6 2000
    863'.64—dc21                                    00-034640

CITY LIGHTS BOOKS are edited by Lawrence Ferlinghetti and
Nancy J. Peters and published at the City Lights Bookstore,
261 Columbus Avenue, San Francisco CA 94133.
Visit our web site: www.citylights.com

# ACKNOWLEDGMENTS

Our appreciation to Éditions Autrement for permission to translate into English and publish the story, "Heart of Skitalietz," which appeared in French translation in *A l'ombre de La Havane*, Paris 1997. The story "Corazón de Skitalietz" was published by Reina del Mar Editores, Cienfuegos, Cuba, 1998. The collection of stories in *A l'ombre de La Havane* will be published in the original Spanish by Ediciones del Bronce, Barcelona, Fall 2000.

This volume marks the first appearance of the author's creative work in English translation. An essay titled "Ojos de La Habana" was translated by Cola Franzen as "Eyes of Havana" and published in *Aperture* 141, Fall 1995.

The appearance of this book in English is the result of a pleasurable, exciting group effort. The translators wish to express heartfelt thanks and gratitude to the author first of all and to Nancy J. Peters and Robert Sharrard at City Lights, who championed this project when it was still a hope, a possibility, a work-in-progress. We are grateful to the author for his lively interest and generous cooperation during all phases of the work, and for his meticulous reading and corrections of the final texts. Thanks also to Mark Schafer and David Davis for careful reading of the translations and for many invaluable suggestions. To Nancy Peters for her expert and sensitive editing of this volume, mil gracias.

["Coming," "A Throw of the Book of Changes," and "Station H" were translated by Dick Cluster. Cola Franzen translated "In the Cold of the Malecón," "This Life," and "Heart of Skitalietz." The work went back and forth between them before the versions were sent to the author.]

# CONTENTS

# COMING

*For Félix Lizárraga*

**His roommate headed for Odessa**, to take a ship back to Havana from there. Of all the possible return routes, this was the longest. He was trying to prolong his time abroad, counting on the sea voyage to let him find reasons that would justify his going back.

"Maybe I'll get shipwrecked," his roommate said, bags already packed. "That could be a piece of luck."

He was left alone in his room in the student dorm, which emptied out little by little. Finally they were down to a small group of Arabs and Cubans who gave up conversing in Russian to seek solace in their private tongues.

He was sorry not to have gone via Odessa. Spreading his bags open on the empty bed, he began to prepare for his return.

In Russia he had gotten used to some customs that he would miss back there. He'd have less freedom, he was sure about that. In September they'd give him his first job and, one way or another, the life it was his lot to live would begin.

With such prospects, he — like the others — roamed rather aimlessly through the empty buildings of the university. He wondered if he'd ever again feel as sheltered as he had during these five years of study.

The Russian summer now seemed matchless, intensifying his pleasure at being in the sun in short sleeves. He bought a few last-minute gifts and finally, when the moment arrived, he picked up his luggage and tried to look happy. If not happy, content.

"It's a deportation," he thought the night before, when he couldn't get to sleep. "I should be staying in Russia."

But he hadn't found the way.

From the first glimpse of the small trees at the airport exit and the slogans in large letters alongside the highway, he had the feeling of being lost in Havana.

"You're home," they told him. "Now nothing, or almost nothing, will seem strange."

The boy he'd been before Russia (when he was studying the Russian language in the preparatory school, and the tour of study abroad awaited him as the culmination of his work) looked out from a table in the living room of his house. He didn't remember putting that photo there. He was thinner in it and had something that now was surely lost: the beauty of anyone between eighteen and twenty, or the fearlessness that naïveté confers.

In Havana, he was like a recently landed spy. He learned the city's customs all over again, made friends, but couldn't find his contact. His mission there was merely to discover a resting place. Then it would be enough to flash a countersign. But to whom?

That's when he knew he was looking for himself.

"Hmpph," he raged inside. "Who needs all that right now?"

His goal was to find the young man in the photograph: daring and uncalculating, lacking in suspicion, but, without a doubt, his contact in Havana.

Then he remembered the diary kept by that boy, the one he'd been six or seven years before.

The teacher lived in a first-floor apartment. He stood outside looking at the slate-blue sea. A ship crossed it so slowly as to seem motionless. That was how his roommate would be sailing, in near-motionlessness like that.

A cat was sleeping by the door. He called it by its name and the cat opened its eyes and went inside through the crack of the half-opened door. Somebody echoed the cat's name in a washed-out voice, the voice of his old teacher.

She had been the first fellow passenger from whom he'd asked directions in Russian. They'd taken the same imaginary train, ordered fantastic soups at a table in an invented Moscow restaurant, walked along boulevards in white nights out of books, been blinded by the tiles of Samarkand. . . . She'd been his best language teacher in the preparatory school.

Now, as always, she had a pupil visiting in her parlor. With him, that made two.

"How nice that you've visited at the same time," she said, introducing them.

The pupil's hair fell like a drizzle over his eyes, and he had braces on his teeth. He'd just finished the preparatory course.

"This was my last year," the teacher explained.

The youngster smiled with the plated smile conferred by the braces. He took part in the conversation through smiles like that, spoke only a few times, and shortly decided to leave.

"I pity him," the teacher said.

He asked why.

"He'll never go to Russia. You know . . ."

No more students would be sent to Russia. That was all over.

"It's all over for you, too," he pointed out.

"Yes, but the difference between that boy and me is that I'd already had enough. I needed an excuse to retire." The teacher lit a cigarette. "And the excuse arrived."

"Yes, it's a shame. To spend a whole year preparing for a trip you don't go on."

"You know, sometimes he's reminded me of you," said the teacher after a silence.

"Who?"

She pointed toward the door with the hand holding her cigarette. Surely he too had prepared himself for something that wasn't going to happen.

"Only he comes alone, not with a girlfriend."

Silence rose up between them, the silence of those who approach an uncomfortable subject. Now he'd have to talk about his girlfriend of those days.

"A friend of hers" — the teacher said the whole name of that friend, because her memory was strong enough to hold onto the names of former students — "told me she hadn't returned."

"She hasn't come back so far."

"Although there's still one ship on the way."

"The one from Odessa."

"And she's probably not coming on it," he supposed.

"How can she manage to stay?"

He shrugged his shoulders, watching the cat go out. He'd come to tell his old teacher so many things, and now he didn't see any point in talking.

"Please pardon this kind of question," she said with some insistence, "but when did you see each other last?"

"A year and then some," he recalled. "We broke up a year or so ago. After that I didn't get much news about her."

The teacher didn't ask about his stay in Russia. Her last course was done.

"In her place I would have done the same," she said. "I would have stayed."

"And what prompted you to come back?" her next question would be.

But she stuck to the same point.

"I think — I know it's nonsense — that she has my phone number, she has my address at this house. . . . Could she know that I'd like to hear from her?"

"I think so," he consoled her. "We talked about you, over there. We remembered you."

The teacher pointed to the cabinet in which she kept the postcards she got, the cards dashed off on the run. Inside the cabinet was a chest, and inside the chest, which had been brought to her by a student who was now a government minister, were the letters and cards.

When he left her house, the ship was so far off it could hardly be seen, and the cat was no longer by the door.

He visited all his favorite old haunts. Some no longer existed, and the others bored him. He looked for friends from back then. They noticed how pale he was and agreed to meet for a day at the beach.

"Except for your color, you're just the same," they assured him.

The picture in the living room could have been taken that same day.

He emptied bookshelves, and the old objects got mixed with those brought from Russia. He came to see that as a good omen, a sign of continuity. A few photos of himself with his girlfriend appeared.

He scoured the apartment without finding his old diary. Maybe someone in his family had recovered it; it could be in his grandparents' house in the provincial city.

"The provincial city," he murmured.

That was memory.

His grandparents' house was smaller than he remembered. It needed paint and masonry work. His grandfather had misunderstood what time he was coming and wasn't ready for him yet.

"You smell of trains and airplanes," was his greeting. "You've experienced so many things."

Smell had replaced grandfather's sight, he was like a blind dog now. His bones and veins seemed to be popping out, leaving the dead skin behind. If he'd hugged him a second time, it was because he was reminded of the other grandson.

"Now your brother would be like you," he said.

The other grandson was his favorite, even if he tried to keep this from being so.

"He'd be older than me."

They sat at a table packed with objects. Open books, half-polished forks, flowers cut but not put in water. Things got finished little by little, as strength or memory allowed.

"I've looked, and it's not here," he explained.

The table top cast doubt on the search.   ·

"But I found this." As a consolation, he handed him a pile of photos.

His brother, with braces on his teeth.

Some smell must have told the old man that things weren't going well. He realized right away that he should take the photos back.

"I thought they were of you," was his excuse. He'd save

them, even if he couldn't tell them apart.

He remembered the pupil visiting his old teacher, the one who wouldn't be going to Russia. In the pictures, his brother had looked a little like that.

"Did you come just for that diary?" the old man asked suspiciously.

He put a sweater into his grandfather's hands.

"I came to bring you my present," he said.

"It's a good one," his grandfather assured him while trying it on.

"It looks good on you."

The distance between the house and sea had lessened. The tree roots were pushing up the terrace floor. Everything lodged in memory got ruined or it shrank. His grandfather had an anachronistic sporty look because the sweater brought back the swimmer he'd once been. Maybe it was a present for a different body, in a different season.

"Aren't you going in the water?" his grandfather asked.

No, he wouldn't swim. They walked along the wet sand.

"Have they offered you a job yet?"

"Not yet."

Then his grandfather asked about her.

"We're not together any more."

"That's too bad."

His steps were surer on the sand than they had been inside.

"Your best days are passing you by," grandfather announced to grandson.

He looked at him, surprised. What could he know of his life?

"Or maybe not," the old man took it back.

He made a motion as if throwing something into the sea. The sweater and the motion were too youthful for him. As if the clothing required certain motions from those who wore it.

In the end, the old man weakened, and gave him the photos again.

Back in his apartment a notice from the post office awaited him.

It informed him of the arrival of a package from Russia, but the name of the sender wasn't on it. Who could still be there, thinking of him? Almost certainly, it had to be her. But he'd have to wait until Monday to be sure.

Putting the photos of his brother with the others, he came upon images of his old girlfriend again.

"Again."

What was happening to him? Nothing was more like his grandfather's table top than he himself. He tried to do things but wasn't able to finish them, he felt he was neither here nor there. Neither in Russia nor in Havana. He was neither his brother nor the pupil he'd met in his teacher's house, nor even the one in the living room photo.

On Monday he recognized the address on the wrapping of the package, the address of a building near the woods in a

17

northern Russian city, far from the city where he'd studied.

From that room you could see the first treetops of the forest and the road between the trunks. The cheap curtains were always open. She held in her hands the collection of letters he had sent.

Smiling, she spread the letters out on the bed. The bed in question was a narrow one in which they slept squeezed together.

"Here you promised me such-and-such," she told him. "In this one you called me a treasure for the first time . . ."

He thought of solitaire, a game that apparently included him, but, in the long run, could not be shared. She tried to wrap herself in words, in a language of love that would serve her as a cloak. He was superfluous there.

She danced around his letters that covered her bed, a crazy joy seeming to inhabit her. In his presence she was revealing a personal and secret rite. The order of the letters implied a vague prediction. In that room near the woods he saw the other side of things.

Now as he gripped the package that had to be holding his letters, he felt the flimsiness of those papers, the flimsiness of her gesture of sending them to Havana. Why, after a year and half without seeing each other, was she sending those letters to him?

He dropped the package among his books and tried to forget about it. He got in touch with her old roommate from that northern city.

"Bring a bathing suit if you want," the girl suggested.

No one seeing her would say she'd come from the cold. Her skin was golden. Strains of music came from somewhere, and the girl asked whether he'd like something to drink.

"Kakoi kricivi pliash!" she yelled from the other end of the house.

Apparently she wasn't yelling at him. The music came from the roof.

"What is it?" he asked about the pink liquid.

"Doctored alcohol," the girl explained.

He raised his eyes toward the ceiling, and she pointed up toward the source of the music.

"Friends. There's so little vacation left . . ."

After the second or third drink he asked about his old girlfriend. He wanted to know what had happened during the year and a half they hadn't seen each other.

"It's a long story, and I don't know the whole thing."

"Tell me what you know."

She took a long swallow.

"It started when you two quarreled. She switched rooms and stopped talking to all her friends. She went to share a room with a Chinese girl from the Soviet Far East. She always liked to act strange."

That sounded like an accusation directed at him, and the accusation came soon enough.

"You filled her head with birds. You made her believe things. But why talk about that now," she added quickly.

19

They drank in the pink alcohol, and the music. Then she stood to reach for a towel and insisted they go up to the roof.

Up there it was the same group as always.

"*Another sunny day on the sands,*" one of them said by way of greeting, as the rest saluted him by raising the suntan oil, the bucket of sea water, a pair of sunglasses.

The girl undressed and asked where his bathing suit was.

"I'm not staying," he explained.

She stared at him for a moment and seemed to be weighing what he'd look like without clothes and with that pale skin.

"You need to," she announced.

She occupied herself rubbing in oil and iodine, and asked him to cover her back with it.

"She got fat," she continued the story. "She ate chocolate around the clock and got really fat."

The sun in his eyes annoyed him.

"She acquired a taste for Indian films and was always in the movies with her chocolates."

"Do you remember the Indian films?" she asked her friends, and the memory amused them.

"I heard she got to like the taste of chocolate wet with her own tears. A really disgusting mix."

"I got a package from her, with the same old address," he said.

The girl with glowing skin looked at him over her sunglasses.

"She wasn't there when we took off," she declared.

"That's all I know."

"How did she manage to stay?" he asked.

"What good would the recipe do you now?" she said. "Now we're here."

The music spoke of love, the sky was clear, and the roof commanded a panoramic view. He looked at her body in the bathing suit.

"Why are you leaving so soon?" the girl asked.

Inside the house, before leaving, he found the bottle and helped himself to more of the pink liquid.


He read the letters that he himself had written two or three years before, when they lived in different Russian cities. He didn't understand what she could see in those papers, some of them written in boredom or annoyance, he knew.

The telephone line diluted the dilute voice of his old Russian teacher even more.

"In one of the letters I found a phrase that isn't Russian," he told her. "She said it while she was asleep, maybe you know what it's about."

"Would you like to say it for me?"

"Anyik kakara anyik kakalma-ra," came out of his mouth.

On the other end of the line the teacher sounded puzzled.

"I don't think it's Russian," she passed judgment after hearing it for the second time. "Not as far as I know . . . . She never told you what it meant?"

"She said she didn't know."

"Well," the teacher seemed to be considering this. "The tongue can utter all kinds of foolishness while we're asleep. Maybe they aren't exactly words."

"It sounded like an insult," he persisted.

"Here's what we'll do," she agreed. "Let me write the phrase down and I promise to look into it."

An empty glass dangled from one of her hands. He pointed at the telephone, also dangling off the hook.

"I was calling you."

He was invited to have a drink.

"Help yourself," she said, and when he was in the kitchen she yelled for him to bring the bottle to the living room.

It took him a while to find a clean glass.

"This color," he said.

"What's wrong with it?"

"It looks like shampoo."

"Don't worry about it."

He poured some pink alcohol for each of them.

"Will it bother you if I hang up the phone?" he asked.

"Why did you come? To wait for a phone call?"

The golden hand hung up the receiver.

"What happened to your friends?"

"Once in a while they remember they have homes. Take off your shoes if you want."

He dropped his shoes on the floor and stretched his legs.

He wasn't wearing socks. Thanks to the alcohol his head began to clear. She began caressing his feet.

"You're so white," she said in a whisper. "Anybody would say you've just come from Russia."

She started to laugh. The phone rang suddenly and she quickly scooped it up.

"Hang it up," he asked quietly.

The golden skin, once she was undressed, had regions that were pale, the white of Russia on her skin.

"Anyik kakara anyik kakalma-ra," he intoned.

The girl broke out laughing on the bed and wrapped herself in the covers.

"What kind of tongue twister is that?" asked her voice from inside her wrapping.

He said he'd heard it in an Indian film.

"Where?"

"In an Indian film."

She sat up.

"It's obvious that you never got anywhere near a theater where they showed even the sorriest Indian film."

Suspecting that the spirit of her old roommate now haunted her bedroom, she scanned the four walls.

"You can't just accept things the way they are, is that it?" she said. "Stop asking questions as if she'd died or been kidnaped. Buried in a movie theater with her tears and her chocolate, what could be better? That's what she decided to do."

He walked toward the door.

"I'm going to find my glass."

"The Indian films," she confided when he got back, "were always dubbed in Russian."

"A beautiful axiom," he remarked, getting under the covers too.

In the Russian whiteness of her skin he found a dark triangle, and in the dark triangle, an entrance. For a good while she called to him as if he were far away, as if she couldn't find him.

"Where does one come from, when one comes?" she asked the ceiling later on.

Where does one come from when one comes?

He was returning again to Havana. He'd been visiting a provincial hospital, where his roommate from Russia was sick. It was a small ward with few beds. Sitting in the visitor's chair he listened to his roommate talk about the last days in Odessa. His mouth moved as if someone were tugging at the corners.

"I saw her there," he insisted.

He looked at the cover of a book on the small metal table.

"What's it about?"

"Spies," the patient said. "A plot about a white slavery network."

He put the book back down on the table.

"She still had a pretty face, but she was a whale."

"In Thailand?"

He pointed at the book. The patient took some time to move one of his limbs.

"All right," he said. "Let's talk about something else."

"How did you end up like this?" he asked to change the subject.

"It's the same story I'm trying to tell you. Her story."

"So tell it. Go ahead. Are you sure it was her?"

"Her clothes made her seem Arabic, or something like that. Maybe it was the earrings or the eye makeup. She'd put it on so thick that if she blinked she'd never be able to open her eyes again."

"And where did you see her?"

"In the shipping office. She said I was wrong, that I had her mixed up with someone else. And she was so fat, it could have been true . . . . Then I saw her in the doorway of a café and I was sure it was her. But when I said her name she denied it. She didn't admit to understanding Spanish."

While trying to change position, he couldn't speak, concentrating all his forces on the movement.

"I thought she'd gone crazy," he picked up the story. "That she didn't know who she was, where she'd come from, and where she had to go back to."

"Maybe she was trying to delay things a little, the way you did," he interrupted.

"No, it wasn't that. I think she was trying to pass for a

foreigner, so as not to have to come back."

The spy novel lost one of its covers as it fell to the floor.

"I took her by the arm at the café door, and then a bunch of guys were all over me."

"What kind of guys?"

"A gang of Arabs."

Judging by his hospitalization, it had been a serious beating.

"So I came home by plane."

"But what was she up to, in all this?"

He began to imagine her caught in a web of white slavers.

"What do I know? In the middle of the fight she started yelling at me."

"What did she yell? Do you remember?"

The sick friend closed his eyes.

"Anyik kakara anyik kakalma-ra?"

He opened them to stare at his visitor.

"What?"

"Did she yell Anyik kakara anyik kakalma-ra?"

The patient smiled through stretched lips.

"No. She just called my mother names."

He broke out laughing too.

"You were the one they wanted to beat up," the patient teased him. "You were lucky not to be in Odessa that day."

He told his friend what had happened with the golden body.

"You should have done that long ago," the patient assured him.

"There was a way to stay, but we didn't know how," he said.

"I'd had enough."

Was that because of Russia, or because of the beating?

"Let go of your nostalgia," his friend said sharply. "That wasn't so marvelous either."

He walked out of the hospital into unknown streets and waited for a night train back to Havana. On the train he fell asleep, and woke up because they had stopped in the middle of the countryside with the engine silenced.

Where do we come from when we come?

He heard some cries that came closer. When they were closer still, he discovered that they made a kind of song. He could hear a current that passed near the train, a current that sounded like a strong river flowing by.

They were cattle being moved during the night, urged onward by the song. As the weak light from the train began to distinguish them, he could just make out hindquarters of cattle and shadows on horseback as they passed.

What the men were singing were the names of the cows. It seemed to him that no song could be better. He got off the train to watch the group of cowboys and cattle recede into the flat land. He heard the whistle of a freight train. A mass of iron passed by them along one flank.

His train signaled that at last it too would get moving,

and for the first time he was sure of having come back. He didn't know where from, or what for. He let the train go, and stayed there alone in the countryside. As happens only in the countryside, the night was absolute. There was no light anywhere, and he thought that, if he hurried, he could catch up with the cattle herd.

# IN THE COLD OF THE MALECÓN

**"He chopped the meat** into small pieces. Too small."

"Like his apartment," the mother commented.

"Yes . . . . And you want to know what I thought, seeing him cut the meat in the kitchen of the tiny apartment?"

She could imagine.

"I thought how strange that we've had a son."

Because they behaved like those old married couples, very attached to one another, who could never have children and in old age each becomes the child of the other.

"It would've been stranger not to have one."

"He was slicing the green bananas into rounds and then removing the skin from each round. You never did it that way."

"No."

She made a pretense of high spirits.

"But the apartment, describe it. What's it like?"

The father began to place all the rooms of the apartment within the room where they were sitting.

"It could all fit in here," he said finally.

"So then he hasn't managed to get away from us," the mother thought.

"And tell me if he ate the meat."

The meat was a present they'd sent him.

"He cooked some of the small pieces and we ate them, and during the meal he talked about his work."

"He told you he'll have to move farther away, right?"

"How'd you guess?"

"It's a pretext of his."

"Could be, yes."

"He needs pretexts to defend himself from us," the mother said aloud.

"Did you see things that weren't his? I mean: does he live alone?"

"There was nobody else with us, no. There was one thing that seemed odd to me."

"What?"

"He didn't want the meat to lose the blood in cooking. He ate it very rare."

"And you?"

"Me? The same as always."

The mother nodded

"While you were eating you asked him to take you to see the whores."

"After we had just finished eating. The pieces of meat were hard to stick a fork into. He asked me what I felt like doing. We had three hours before my train left and could take advantage of the time."

"Go on. Go on."

"Near his apartment are some movie theaters. Or we could walk around a little . . . . Then I told him I'd like to see the whores again."

"See them again?" The mother burst out laughing. "They can't be the same ones, they'd be wrecks by now."

The father laughed too.

"Of course."

"He knows where to find them," the mother mused aloud.

"He said we could go but that it was a bad night to walk along the Malecón. We might not find any."

"Why a bad night?"

"The surf. The waves crash over the top of the wall of the Malecón. You can't stay there without getting splashed."

"But finally you did find some."

"After a lot of walking. They were on the edge of the side-walk, being careful of the waves and looking at the cars passing by."

"And they didn't look at you?"

The father suddenly felt ridiculous.

"At me? I'm old."

"At him."

"One woman looked at him for a moment. Just a moment, that's all. Like when you mistake someone in the street and realize the mistake immediately."

"And then?"

"She went back to looking at the street so she wouldn't

33

miss any cars."

"Keep going."

"And that was all. We went back to his apartment to have coffee. I really liked the coffee, it gave me a lift. I asked him if he'd seen how that woman had looked at him."

"Yes."

"And in spite of how strange it was being his father, it felt right, the two of us in the nice warmth of his apartment, the two of us there and those women outside in the cold of the Malecón."

There the story ended. The two old people were silent for a while.

"Tell me again," the mother asked.

"What do you want me to tell you?"

"The way she looked at him, the woman you found."

The tufts of hair lie at the edge of the patio and the older brother, scissors still in hand, observes how they disappear bit by bit. The wind mixes the hair with the fallen leaves of the casuarinas (they call these trees pines) that seem like tufts of thicker and more brittle hair.

Leaves and hair form ethereal balls that hover among the half-exposed roots.

"Those are the souls of the hair that's been cut," he'll explain to his brother as soon as he comes out of the water.

The younger one persists in practicing the backstroke. He splashes awkwardly, still lacking rhythm in the stroke of his arms.

One day he'll teach him. The day he decides to go back in the water. Because he's lost his taste for swimming in the sea, and spends most of the day on the patio, in the shade.

The people in the area, mostly seasonal guests, are intrigued by this boy who cares so little for the summer that's coming to an end.

They hear him dash by at night on his bicycle like a gust of wind and wonder where he can be going.

A few tufts of hair swirl around the chair on the patio. He

puts the scissors on the chair and whistles toward the beach.

The second time he whistles louder.

In the water the younger one's upraised arm changes from a part of his stroke to a gesture of protest.

The dark cloud that covers the horizon is moving in.

In the garden (the garden grows on sand and so it is thin), the shower does not work. There's a bucket under it, and in the bucket floats a dipper. Though he'd like to, the younger brother can't dump the whole bucket of water on himself at once.

He pours three or four dippers and stops. The dipper half-floats on the surface, taking on water slowly until it sinks to the bottom.

On the calm surface of the bucket is the reflection of the cloud.

The patio door bangs shut, but not because the older one has gone in. The older brother sits down in the chair and pulls the scissors out from under one thigh.

The younger one jumps up and down from the cold. The dripping water makes a shadow at his feet on the patio floor.

The younger brother starts to do windmills with his arms, assuring the elder that the water was warm.

He always bring news of the beach. He thinks that his brother's is not the final word.

The older one takes note of his wet head. As the first drops fall, they go in. The chair stays outside.

The previous night they invented a strange game: one rearranges the furniture (beach-house furniture is light in weight) for the other's return. The older brother leaves his bicycle outside, comes into the completely dark house, and has to find his way among the furniture.

If he doesn't bump into anything, he wins.

Seated on one of the chairs, in the darkest corner, the younger one keeps his ears open for any noise. If he wins, his brother has to teach him the backstroke.

The older brother has complained of how foreseeable everything is. For instance, walking in the dark among the furniture, when habit keeps one from bumping into anything.

The game the two of them are playing grows out of this complaint.

Coming home the previous night (having left the younger one to his chessboard), he finds the house dark among the casuarinas (which they call pines).

The arrangement of the furniture has been changed, and he touches the first piece in the dark. It's a chair (the one now getting wet on the patio) and he goes on from it to a table and from the table to some shelves. He manages at last to reach the goal, the electric switch on the wall.

The light shows that the changes amount only to a rotation of things.

Everybody knows how useful it is to rearrange furniture. We rearrange it because we've brought a new object into the family, or because we can't bring one in. To accommodate everybody who can fit at the party, or because nobody comes.

Anyone who's done it often knows that these changes consist mainly of a rotation of things. The room's walls remain fixed, while the contents revolve. The furniture, the objects, and those who live among them have one day's advantage over the four walls.

At the end of this time period, the illusion runs out. Then the things look the same as before, mated to the room.

Breaking down the order we've given to the furniture turns out to be very difficult to do. The furnishings do not seem disposed to allow the old relationships to be broken. They cling to each other so nobody can pull them apart. The bookshelf grabs hold of the chair, and the bed grabs the mirror.

When we set out to make changes in a room, what we will surely attain is a change in the orientation of the existing relationships. The same relationship exists between objects and walls as between the needle and face of a compass.

A true change would be changing the walls. Or giving it all up and leaving the room behind.

The house is darkened by the cloud and the surrounding trees.

It's early, but they've turned on the lights. The younger brother plays at his chessboard, alone. The older one is watching the rain. The glass in the patio door shows the chair getting wet.

The rain makes the chair stand out as if it would signify something. There it rests.

Several afternoons go by like this. The parents telephone every evening and speak of the sick man who has not yet died. One night they decide that if the situation doesn't improve (the solution is the patient's death) the father will return to the beach house.

It's the end of summer.

At night, they play that strange game that the younger one has invented, a kind of the chess with objects.

The younger brother has begun to break the established relations among the furniture. Every night he comes closer to perfecting his chaos.


The last night (they know the father will arrive the next day) the older brother looks at the clear sky.

Sprawled on the grass, the bicycle at his side, he listens to the sound of the waves.

He confirms that the sky has changed considerably in a short time (summer is ending) and that the destiny of all things is to revolve.

(Whoever discovers this, that everything is a large room where change consists only of rotation, grows sad.)

He takes the bicycle and dashes between the houses. The people in the area, principally seasonal guests, wonder where that gust of wind could be coming from.

When he arrives, the house is dark among the trees and the younger brother is waiting inside.

He leaves the bike outside, pushes the door and moves into the dark.

Everything is foreseeable. To walk in the darkness between the pieces of furniture until, before reaching the goal, his hands touch a door that's never been there before.

He searches for the switch. Not finding it, he thinks for a minute. Then he puts a hand on the doorknob, and opens the door.

The wind carries balls of hair and leaves, but the trunks of the trees are missing. This is not the garden. He takes a few steps and the wind settles down. The balls float. He has forgotten to tell his brother their true nature. But it doesn't matter, he advances among the souls.

# STATION H

Railroad station H lies halfway between two cities. As seen on a map, it more or less exactly marks the midpoint between the capital and the next city. There is no other building in the area (the closest stands two kilometers off). The place comes alive only when trains meet.

At other times, the small building at Station H is merely a landmark on the railway line, one of those points indicated at intervals on maps. It signifies a moment when two trains converge there.

A buzzer sounds on one wall of the small building, the conductors of both trains pick up metal cases like toolboxes, and they sound their whistles in answer to the station buzzer. As the trains depart, those who may have stayed behind on the platform must close their eyes against the onslaught of the sun. If, that is, anyone should take it into their head to stay behind at Station H.

Passengers do get off for a few minutes to stretch their legs, but even this doesn't happen very much. Instead they keep busy observing the passengers on the other train, with the indulgent attitude of those who have already completed the portion of the voyage that the others are only now beginning, the indulgence with which an old person regards a child.

But those who take a few strides along the platform and drink from the water fountain built into the wall of the station may discover, beneath the iron smell of the trains, a discreet odor of coffee. And from this odor it is possible to deduce that Station H does have some existence outside the moment when the trains converge.

Once the station empties, the office workers have a bit more than two hours of idle time, which allows them to get out of the office and assemble in the adjoining coffee shop. Then real coffee is brewed (for the passengers, it's in scarce supply), and they talk about life two kilometers away, where the first houses appear.

Like the coffee, the conversation tries to squeeze as much juice as possible from a very few things. During these dead hours nothing comes to Station H, not even sounds (the measures taken to save electricity make it impossible to listen to the radio), and after noon it becomes essential to have coffee every once in a while.

One morning an elderly man arrived at Station H on the train from the capital. An elderly man is not the kind of passenger who stretches his legs, has a drink from the fountain, or downs a quick cup of coffee. Age robs one of daring, and older passengers are almost always worried that the train may leave them behind.

There are cases of those who, in the middle of the trip, feel that they shouldn't go on and so, in order to retrace their course, change trains at Station H. The elderly man was not among those stunned or superstitious ones. He stood without moving for a moment, studying the train across the platform as if he were looking for someone.

His expression didn't say much. His face had the air of those faces that we don't really recognize among our old family photos. His clothes didn't reveal much either, just the kind of cloudy impression given by clothes that have seen a lot of use. Nothing about him demanded attention except the fact of his having gotten off the train, in no hurry, at such a whistlestop. Except a thin wooden box that he carried.

The elderly man placed his box on one of the tables of the coffee shop. These tables seemed out of place, given the lack of space in the room and the nature of the station. Only quite rarely did passengers find the time to sit down to drink their coffee, and no one there had ever seen such patience as that now being shown by this elderly man. The woman in charge of the coffee shop took pleasure from being one up on the men from the office. She was the only one to witness the old man's arrival.

She asked whether he wanted to order anything, but received a shake of the head. The conductor of one of the trains came in to hand her a folded note. The buzzer sounded outside, and the conductor left. Without unfolding the paper yet, the woman looked at the elderly man.

"The trains are leaving," she warned.

The man looked out as if he were expecting someone

who hadn't arrived, and asked what time the trains would converge again.

"In three more hours."

One train whistled, and then the other. The two iron accordions creaked and clattered, and Station H was again full of sun. The light came in through the windows and through the coffee shop door. Motes of dust floated in the light. They took their time in falling. Some of them came to rest on the old man's shoes.

"You could change tables."

The woman knew the ebb and flow of the light within the coffee shop.

"The sun will shine there soon," she warned.

The elderly man took his box to another table. On his hands were the same spots that time deposits on all old things.

The telephone rang. It would ring two or three more times and then the office staff would come to sit at the tables. The coffee shop woman decided she'd have to hurry to find out more about the elderly man.

"He came from the capital," she told herself, "but where is he going? Nobody comes to visit here at Station H."

He went out onto the platform, and the woman was able to take a good look at his box. The wooden cover had a checkerboard design.

One of the office workers stuck his head in the window.

"What's that guy up to?" he asked.

She pointed to the box and the office worker leaned further inside.

"A chessboard."

When he came back, the old man moved the box, as if someone had touched it while he'd been gone.

"Good morning," said the man from the office, and the older man answered his greeting.

"Did your train leave without you?"

The elderly man looked at the man from the office and shook his head.

"I'm waiting for the next ones."

"Here we come," the man from the office said to the coffee shop woman.

That was his coded way of telling her to make a pot of coffee as strong as could be managed. The elderly man sensed the woman observing him.

"Have you seen another box like this around here?" he suddenly asked.

She looked at the box as if she hadn't seen it before.

"With squares like this." He pointed to the checkerboard pattern. "Hasn't there been anybody here with a box like this?"

"I don't think so."

The man sighed and untied his shoes. His ankles were swollen.

"Are you looking for somebody with a box like that?"

He nodded.

"Here?" It was difficult for her to recover from her surprise.

"By now he should be here. He should have come in the train that met mine," the elderly man confirmed.

The woman found it hard to believe that two city people would have made such a date in the coffee shop where she worked. The first of the office workers came in. Then the woman started to read the sheet of paper the conductor had given her.

When she had finished reading it, she noticed the change that had taken place. The box was spread on the table; it had grown. Coming closer, she saw how it worked: it opened on hinges.

"Do you want to play?" the elderly man asked the woman in charge of the coffee shop.

The coffee pot whistled and the men from the office took their places at the tables.

"Would one of you like to play?" The elderly man extended his invitation to those who had just arrived.

The only one who knew how to play chess was the man who came to meet the night trains. The woman put less coffee than usual in each glass, and put one glass on each table. The last one was for the visitor.

The elderly man neither paid nor said thank you. Flies buzzed around his coffee. He moved a white piece and then a black one. The black pieces were on the far side, and his hand touched them with a different flair.

Each time he made contact with the black figures, the old man pretended to be the opposing player.

"Is the person you're waiting for coming to play with you?" the coffee shop woman dared to asked.

He answered yes.

One of the men from the office asked whether they could play checkers, and the others moved their chairs in closer. The woman moved away from the group.

"What's he like, the person you're waiting for?" she asked.

"He's coming with a box like this. We agreed to meet here for a game."

"But is he tall or short? Thin or fat? Does he have hair or is he bald?" The coffee shop woman acted out each characteristic, as if the old man's memory might have lost track of someone.

The old man shrugged.

"I don't know."

"Ah. So you don't know him?"

"Not yet. We've been playing for a year but we haven't seen each other."

She thought he was talking about someone nonexistent, about his own hand touching the black pieces.

"How can that be?" asked the elderly man's opponent in the checkers game.

"We play by letter," he answered. "By mail. We were going to meet here, at the halfway point."

It annoyed him, to spoil chess with a game of checkers like this.

"When I left home I wasn't sure what we'd decided about the board, so I brought this one. I was afraid of getting this far and their coming too, and our not having any chessmen."

The man from the office won, and the elderly man gathered the pieces, dumped them off the board, and began to put them away.

The woman pitied him.

"Should I heat it up?" she asked about the coffee he hadn't touched.

He thanked her and said he wasn't going to drink it. So the office staff shared out his coffee in equal parts, and as soon as the old man left the coffee shop, they took up the topic of the dead.

A few days earlier, they had found blood by the office door.

"It had to be a wounded animal," the checkers player declared.

"And it came right to the door."

"It came right to the door, yes. That's where there's the most light at night. It came to lie down under the lights."

The coffee shop woman turned on the water faucet, and the men kept quiet.

"The dead," they said at last, reluctantly.

She placed the clean glasses on the counter.

"Which of you is feeling remorse about an accident?" the one who seemed to be the boss asked the others.

"An accident?"

"Have we been guilty of some death? Does one of you feel remorse for some mistake?"

No one, even if they felt it, was disposed to admit the fact.

"Answer!" the boss demanded.

"No. Not at all," answered the checkers player.

"Then why did you all invent this idea that the dead were coming to the office to square accounts?"

"It wasn't us who invented any of that," they all began to defend themselves.

The boss still didn't seem satisfied.

"No. I know very well who's been making it up."

He was talking about the man who came to meet the night trains. The checkers player slid his thumb along the cover of the chess box. The wood squeaked.

The boss went out onto the platform to smoke, but the cigarette tasted bad and he threw it on the track without smoking it.

"The old man is asleep on a bench," he announced when he returned to the coffee shop.

The woman was reading the letter the conductor had brought.

"Look at her," somebody teased. "She's playing chess by mail too."

The coffee shop woman slapped him with a rag and put the letter away.

"Don't leave us, *chica,*" the men begged as they laughed.

The train conductor would arrive soon. She went to sit on the edge of the platform. She found a lit cigarette by the tracks and smoked for a bit. The office workers laughed and raised their voices once in a while. The elderly man slept further down, on one of the cement benches.

The office telephone rang and somebody ran to answer it. The coffee shop woman got up to make the coffee for the trains.

She wiped the tables, put the elderly man's chess set on the counter, and noticed she was missing a glass.

"None of us took a glass," they told her in the office.

Now they didn't have any time for her. But someone had broken a glass or stolen it, and they'd better not hold her responsible.

The telephone rang again. The train from the capital was running late, so the other train would have to wait for it at Station H. The coffee shop woman saw that the elderly man had changed position in his sleep. She put the water on to boil, and the boss came to tell her not to worry about the glass.

"But if he has a newborn child . . . ," he pointed out to her.

The woman touched a corner of the chess box.

"You're married too," she said.

"It's not the same. You know that."

The boss tried to take her hand but she pulled it away.

"I don't want to know anything. Leave me alone."

She turned on the water faucet. He said something, and she turned off the stream of water so she could hear what it was.

"I said they won't deduct the glass from your pay," repeated the boss.

The coffee shop woman unfolded the letter to assure herself of something, she didn't know quite what. The water boiled, the coffee was ready, and the station buzzer signaled the arrival of the first of the trains. The sound of iron wheels drew close and the station was hidden from the sun.

A passenger came into the coffee shop with a boy. After glancing all around, he saw the box.

"Where's the owner?" the man asked.

The woman in charge of the coffee shop had to keep the boy from dumping the pieces onto the counter.

"Are you the one who came to play with him?" she asked the man.

The boy shook his head violently until his father made him stop.

"He's here, isn't he?" the father asked.

The coffee shop woman nodded.

"Out there. He lay down on a bench and fell asleep, but the train must have woken him up. He's probably in the bathroom. He's an elderly man."

The man took the boy by the hand, and the boy tried to take the chess box with him.

"Do you play too?" the coffee shop woman asked as she lifted the box from his hands.

The boy sprang, facing the woman, almost eye to eye with her.

"It's me who plays," he informed her with an unusually serious voice for a seven-year-old.

The coffee shop woman looked at the father.

"Come on, don't be in a bad mood," said the father, taking the boy outside.

She thought nobody in his right mind would travel an hour and half to play a game of chess with someone that small. Father and son came back to the coffee shop soon. The man asked for a cup of coffee.

"I want one too," the boy announced.

"Two then." The father resigned himself but did not seem to be in a good mood.

"Did you find him?" the woman in charge of the coffee shop asked.

"Yes."

The woman asked how old the boy was.

"Six," answered the father.

"Seven," the boy, standing next to the chess box, contradicted him right away.

"He'd like to be seven now," the father explained. "His birthday is next month."

The coffee shop woman looked at the boy.

"You don't need to be in such a hurry," she advised.

She thought that having such an intelligent child must be a burden.

"Drink your coffee and stay still, okay? If you're not going to play you don't need to touch the box."

"But I like this set better than mine," the boy declared.

"If you like it better," reasoned the father, "then we could agree that the winner of the game gets to keep this set."

The boy jumped up, put his elbows on the counter, closed his eyes, and considered his father's offer.

"You'd beat him easily," his father's voice promised him. "You just have to imagine that you don't have such an older man across from you. Pretend that we're writing him one of our letters. Let's wake him up. Come on." The father led the boy to a table.

She would have sworn that the tables were all clean, but nonetheless the boy was spreading water around with a fingertip. He came back to the counter to touch the box again.

"That man came all the way here to play with you," the coffee shop woman explained to him in a very quiet voice.

The boy looked her in the eye.

"He's a very old man. Traveling is hard for him. You and your father were late, and now you want to leave. Think about him, okay?"

"It doesn't matter now that he'll find out your age," the father said from his table. "We're here now."

The boy's intent eyes fixed on those of the woman in charge of the coffee shop again.

"Men have to face up to things," she pronounced.

Then the boy lifted up six fingers, one for each year.

"I'm a boy, not a man."

"You're a chess player." The father pulled him back to the table again. "A chess player, yes or no?"

At least he answered yes to this. His father tried again to convince him to play. The boy listened for a good while, then practically exploded, shouting, "I'm telling you, that old man is going to die."

The father and the coffee shop woman exchanged a look. The station buzzer sounded and the boy ran outside. His father called after him to be careful. He asked for more coffee.

"Do you have children?" he asked the woman in charge of the coffee shop.

"Three."

"So you know how they are."

Station H got darker than it had been. The conductor of the late train hurried into the coffee shop with his metal case. She served two cups of coffee and asked about the cause of the delay.

"The usual." He looked at her before taking a swallow from the glass. "So?" he asked.

The coffee shop woman put the letter on the counter, her open palm on top of it.

"Tell me it's no lie."

"Of course not."

His hand covered her hand on the letter.

"Okay, but tell me."

"It's no lie."

The station buzzer announced the departure of the trains, and the conductor had to leave on the run without finishing his coffee.

"I'm off duty after the next train. Wait for me," he urged the coffee shop woman.

She watched him toss his box ahead of him and climb on board the moving train. The coffee shop woman could not find the elderly man in the station. She asked the men in the office whether they had seen him get on either train, but none of them knew what to say. So she gave the chess set to the man who waited for the night trains.

"You're the only one it's any use to," she said.

The last trains arrive at Station H a little past midnight. The radio is on, transmitting with the intensity of a fire glowing in a jungle camp.

In the predawn hours, there's nobody in the station. Station H is a point on the map of the electrical engineers. Insects, seeking light at all hours, hover around it. In summertime crickets fly nearby and fight, and behind them come frogs and toads. A dog or a wild cat may come by, and leave quickly because of the smell that people have left behind.

That's all.

The imagination insists that there are nights when the railroad's dead gather there. At night, the small, lit-up building is not ghostly enough. The dead come to the office to lodge their protests, to blame their deaths on the office workers.

Crossroads, even those of railroads, favor ghosts and witchcraft. Two trains cross and time is frozen or annulled. Seeing them from the platform of Station H, then, one could consider oneself a ghost.

# THIS LIFE

*For Rebeca Chávez*

Every day she traveled on that train from one province to another.

She'd insulted a boss. On top of that she'd had the nerve not to apologize. Then they told her she'd have to clear out, that there'd be no job for her anywhere in the province. That's how her travels began.

At first she'd slept with the guys who worked in the dining car. There were three of them. One wore glasses, the second dyed his hair, and the third was just a kid.

After some months, they must have gotten bored or started to feel she had a right to travel without a ticket. They no longer asked her for anything in exchange.

One of those evenings on the way home from work, Cora found the dining car empty. No passengers in it and not even anybody preparing meals. She walked the length of the car and saw a half-filled bottle and a glass on one of the tables.

At another time of her life she would have thought it was a beautiful evening. The landscape scurrying past, the light that precedes the coming of summer. She threw her shoes into her bag and put her feet up. She had only that one pair of shoes, the bag was old and the leather scuffed, making it look splotched with grease. She closed her eyes and before long was nodding off.

When she woke up, a man in pajamas was massaging her feet. She called him doctor. After such an exhausting day a foot massage felt very good.

The man in pajamas was not a doctor but a veterinarian. Or perhaps a veterinarian's assistant. In any case it had been a long time ago. She looked at the man's eyes, the bags under his eyes.

"Whose could these belong to?" she asked gesturing toward the bottle and the glass.

He finished the massage.

"There now, your feet are like a child's. Incredible, as if you'd hardly walked at all in your whole life."

The floor had been swept but not scrubbed, and the dirt of many trips remained. Cora took her shoes out of her bag and went to sit at the table with the bottle.

The evening light came in through the windows. The evenings were beginning to grow longer now. The dining car crew didn't allow her or the doctor to go to another car. They were traveling without tickets on condition they not move from there.

The doctor came to sit across from Cora again. In pajamas and tennis shoes he looked as if he'd been snatched from his house, kidnapped as he sat watching television.

In one gulp she downed half the glass.

"How're things?"

He responded with a gesture that meant: "Same as always."

The door of the car opened and in came a man neither of them knew. His head was shaved. Without looking at them, he picked up the bottle and glass.

The doctor asked him where he'd gotten on the train; he mentioned the stop at the prison.

"Did you see the three guys who work here?"

The man with the shaved head had made the bottle vanish.

"Someone slipped into the car where the electrical unit is and they went to find him," he added.

They heard boisterous voices coming from the next car and a small black man entered stepping as if in military review.

"Felipe!" the doctor burst out laughing. "It was you traveling in the electrical unit?"

The small black man was barefoot, and wore military clothing stolen from the laundry of some encampment. Behind him came the dining car crew.

"At ease!" they ordered.

Felipe took advantage of the fact that they were greeting Cora and the doctor and sat down across from the man who was drinking alone. He believed he'd found in that stranger a kindred soul and reached with lemur fingers for the glass.

"Private Felipe!" shouted the man with the dyed hair, and the small black man leapt from his seat. "Attention!"

"We're not open today," they advised the man with the shaved head. "There's nothing to eat."

He lifted his glass in a sign of peace: a tranquil drunk would cause no trouble.

"Where are you going, Felipe?"

The small black man answered with a vague gesture.

"Answer the doctor!" ordered the man with the dyed hair. "In words. You know how to talk."

"Over there.

"Over there," he repeated.

"The same place as you, doctor," said the one wearing glasses.

Felipe gazed at the same distant point military formations look at. Or toward where his journey was heading, without knowing where for sure.

"I'm hungry," he complained.

"Felipe is hungry," said the three of the dining car crew.

"March!" they ordered at once.

They opened the door to the refrigerator room.

Cora and the youngest of the three had gone in there one afternoon. The atmosphere was sticky and your skin got covered with fine salt from the walls.

Felipe marched with determined steps to the door.

"Forward!" they ordered him.

Stopping at the entrance, he examined the interior for a moment. There was no food inside, it was empty. This could not be his journey's destination. But they gave him a hard shove and closed the door.

They waited a moment in case he gave some signals from inside, but nothing from inside reached them.

"Boys . . . ," began the doctor and they reassured him with the news that the refrigerator wasn't working.

They also ruled out the possibility of asphyxiation. Hadn't he tried to ride in the electrical unit of the train? Now they had him shut him up in a much safer space.

"He'll sleep inside there until we arrive," the man with the dyed hair assured them.

"But he didn't say where he was getting off," the doctor continued to defend him.

Over there . . . . What could over there mean in Felipe's head?

"He doesn't have a ticket," warned the youngest of the three with eyes fixed on Cora and the doctor.

They were nearing a station. They didn't have tickets either.

"He can travel to the end of the line, but inside there."

They stopped at a platform jammed with passengers and a few managed to get on board. Cora and the doctor saw the anxiety of those left on the platform. They would spend the night there, and perhaps tomorrow . . .

From inside the refrigerator room came a few little bangs. The station was left behind, and they heard more desperate blows.

"Kick the door," Cora demanded in her head. "You have hard feet, animal hooves."

After a short time Felipe stopped banging. The youngest man put his ear to the wall of the refrigerator room. He tried to open it only a hair and immediately the tips of lemur fingers grasped the door frame.

"The monster's coming out!" warned the man wearing glasses in the midst of their laughter.

They held the door against Felipe's thrusts.

"That's enough now," said the man with the shaved head.

The dining car crew turned toward him.

"Let him out now."

Felipe managed to get an arm out.

"Mind your own business, brother," advised the man wearing glasses.

They bent Felipe's arm until they made him howl. The doctor stood up.

"Hey, boys, don't fool around like that."

One of them closed the door of the refrigerator room again and the crew shot a triumphal glance at the stranger.

"And you, do you have a ticket?" they asked.

They heard Felipe whimpering. The stranger with the shaved head put a piece of paper on the table.

"You have a ticket, but not to travel in this car," explained the youngest of the three. "Go to your seat and get rid of that bottle."

"There's no bottle." The stranger gestured at the bare table. "Let him out."

"Listen, we don't want a hassle in here," warned the dining car crew. "You'd better go."

"I'm going," he said as he stood up, "but open the door for him."

He waited a moment in the aisle. Felipe began to bawl and kick the door. The dining car crew went for the stranger who suddenly produced a bottle and smashed it on the edge of the table. A rain of glass paralyzed the three.

The refrigerator room door squeaked as the doctor opened it.

"Stop horsing around!" he said.

The man with the shaved head swept the glass toward the wall with one of his boots. The boots were shiny, new.

"Come out of there, Felipe," ordered the doctor.

Felipe didn't want to know what was waiting for him outside.

"Forward march, soldier!" shouted the man with the dyed hair.

The small black man appeared, his nose running and eyes full of tears. One of his feet was bleeding, but he kept the cadence of the march.

"Nothing serious," the doctor commented after glancing at his foot.

"You should have been a veterinarian, doctor."

Without ceasing to march, Felipe sniffed hard, dried his eyes on the sleeve of his military jacket. They ordered him to halt.

Then, with heels together and looking straight ahead, he began to urinate. The spot on his pants grew larger, as unintentionally as if he were urinating in a dream. The urine soaked his bare feet and made the wound burn. But he tried not to lose his military posture.

It was so ridiculous that the man with the shaved head burst out laughing as he watched. Cora, the doctor, and all of them began to laugh.

"Something's broken," said one of the three when, all of a sudden, the motors stopped.

And that made them laugh harder. It was as if they'd all urinated.

They raced off the train arm in arm. Almost at the bottom of the embankment, she fell onto the cushion of grass and he fell on top of her. The doctor's heart was beating wildly and he was gasping for air.

"Cora," he murmured.

"What?"

Cora concentrated on the pattern the threads made in the material of his pajamas. The doctor let himself fall back onto the grass.

"This life."

Lying side by side they again clasped hands.

"I worked, educated my children. My wife died before I reached the age of retirement. Every evening the train would pass and I would say to myself: Soon you're going to leave, bound for no place in particular."

He took a breath before finishing.

"Then they discovered my illness and I went from work to hospitals. There was no retirement. There's never any retirement."

"You know what my older son wants me to do?" he asked.

Cora did not seem to be listening to him.

"To leave him a note saying where I'm going."

In the sky a cloud was spreading.

"People who hang themselves leave notes," said the doctor. "At least they know where they're going."

The wind pushing the clouds along in the sky made the grass around them wave. For an instant they thought they were floating. At the foot of the slope lay a valley and then some hills and behind them would be other valleys all the way to the sea.

Felipe passed close by eating a guava.

"Felipe! Where did you find that guava?"

The small black man immediately hid the fruit. Everything he had — a train trip, a piece of fruit, a jacket — he got on the sly.

"Where are you going, soldier?" asked the doctor coming near him.

A lemur finger pointed to the other side of the train.

"The river," said Felipe, and the doctor went with him.

A train arrived from the other direction and the mechanics gathered around the broken engine. Later the second train left with the dining car crew on board. They saw the doctor and Felipe in the river and shouted out several jokes to them.

"He can't come on board again," commented the one wearing glasses, referring to the doctor. "In case he should die on us in pajamas and without a ticket."

They saw Cora lying on the grass and thought about how old she had become in a short time.

The moon appeared in the sky that was once again clear. On the bank of the river Cora found the doctor's pajamas folded over the tennis shoes. The branches of the trees were leaning over the water. She called that their train was now ready to leave, heard a splashing, and the doctor's head emerged from among the branches.

"Are you touching bottom?" she asked the head.

"It's divine. Try it."

"It's my train."

She said "my train" the same way she would have said "my life, my house, my work."

"Cora's leaving, Felipe."

Even in the water, the small black man was still wearing his military jacket.

"Okay," he turned his back to the shore, and again disappeared among the branches. "Let her go."

She met the man with the shaved head in the last light of the day. There was no electricity in the dining car and they were alone. He poured alcohol from another bottle into his hands and wiped them over his face. She saw him grit his teeth, and was surprised that he had a new bottle and a wound.

"What happened to you?"

Half of his face was in shadow, and the wound on the dark half.

"It was them, no?" she pointed toward the refrigerator room as if the dining car crew were in there, about to beat him up.

"I don't have a glass anymore," was the man's only reply.

Cora took a big slug from the bottle and suddenly touched the man's chin, turning his face toward the light.

"It was the bone," he explained.

He proved to be so invincible that nobody could wound him. If he had a wound, it came from inside, from one of his bones. She asked him where he got so many bottles.

"I was saving them."

"Did you spend a lot of time inside?"

He said yes and moved his legs from under the table.

"I also got these boots." His feet were hard to see in the darkness of the car.

"They're good ones, tough. I knew I was going to need them."

She assumed he'd had to fight for them.

"And where are you coming from?" he asked.

"From work."

He looked outside for an instant.

"Then, where are you going?"

"Back home."

"You work a long way off," he commented. "There's no work nearer by?"

"For me, no."

"It's my prison," she was about to answer him. She had made a prison the same way he had made his wound: from inside, out of pride, to feel invincible.

"Why were you in prison?"

"For killing a woman."

She continued with her questions:

"What woman?"

"Mine."

Cora remained silent, not daring to touch the bottle.

"Did you have children?"

"No."

Neither did she. There was something sad about not having children. They drank the rest and he put another bottle on the table. Cora burst out laughing.

"It seems like magic."

"It is magic," he caressed the neck of the full bottle.

Neither of them had any matches. She would have liked to show him the photo she kept in her bag. Every time she drank she tried to get people to identify her with the girl in that photo.

She pressed her head so strongly against his that she caused the pain in his cheek to flare up, reminding him of his injury.

The man with the shaved head looked toward the horizon that had to be there outside these walls, indistinguishable in the night.

"Those three . . ." he swore.

And to her they seemed so distant, those three men from the dining car. As if the train were not going to pass by on another day, or as if that regular routine of the journey were no longer part of her life.

Her arms still around him, she begged him to forget the fight. This was, after all, his first day of freedom. Now he must try to be free.

# HEART OF SKITALIETZ

**Some guests were gazing** down at the spectacle of the open bay, and he, who was alone, spoke for himself:

"I'd like to live in such a city, I'd be delighted to stay in this one."

He left the garden and the wedding celebration without waiting for whatever food they were going to serve, crossed several dark streets, and came to a small apartment from which the sea could not be seen. Because, in spite of the desire he'd just expressed, he lived in that same city.

He had to decide now what to do next, to continue the work of filling out more and more file cards or to take some pills and sleep for a week. Either of those two possibilities would enable him to make it to another Saturday without dwelling on things too much. Next weekend she would not be there to call him, and after her honeymoon she would have flown away.

He was about to take the first pill when the telephone rang, sounding odd.

"I don't think she could be calling," he thought with joy and sadness.

But now, he heard two women talking on the phone and started to listen in. One seemed to be reading predictions and advice to the other, the horoscope for the coming week from a foreign magazine.

"And me, what am I going to do that week?" he thought, holding the receiver in one hand and the pill in the other, when it occurred to him to join in the conversation. He asked what the magazine said about Scorpios.

"Scorpios," one of the voices repeated.

"Crossed wires," said the other in a resigned voice. "Hang up."

The first explained that there was no magazine at all.

And where was all he'd heard about astrological signs coming from?

"There's no magazine, Scorpio, I'm an astrologer."

"Come on, come on," scolded the other.

It seemed to him that this whole business was more than mere chance.

"One moment," he insisted. "I need to see you, tell me when, the sooner the better.

"What!" the other voice exploded, but he managed to hear what the astrologer said: "Come see me tonight if you wish."

Crossing streets in the middle of a blackout delays any trip, and it was hard to find a street and number in such darkness. Since he'd have to climb the stairs, he took a deep breath. On the door he found a card that was noticeable even in the dark. There was a painted flower, also a scar, some vertical lips, and a blood-stained sword.

"Scorpio," she called him again.

He didn't know the way in nor could he see her, but the astrologer asked him to take a seat just where he was, on a sofa. They talked a bit about the blackout, about when the lights would come back on. The woman was sitting on a high seat, like a bar stool. He could see her only as a shape.

"Did you mind my calling you Scorpio?"

Something in her voice was different now.

"It took me so long to get here that the waiting has put her in a bad mood," he thought.

"Which Scorpio are you going to be?" she asked mostly for herself. "Do you like old things, vintage cars, antiques, old movies, second-hand books, used clothing?"

"Worn-out sheets," she went on, "older women, ancient songs, news that's no longer news?"

He laughed at that last remark and told her he was a historian.

Eyes opened in the cushion his elbow was resting on and the cushion turned into a cat.

"Historian?" asked the cat in a very clear voice.

"Then you will have wondered before," continued the animal, "what do people do to keep on living?"

"What do they turn to? Dear God, the pills!" he thought, looking into the cat's eyes, those eyes that were the only thing visible in the house.

What time was it when he took the first pill, if he'd actually taken it? And how many were necessary to cause a cat

83

to go on talking to him?

He looked for the shape of the astrologer in the darkness, but it was no longer on the stool; it complained from a little farther away:

"How can I bear this consulting day after day without getting sick? So many people without even a peephole to catch a glimpse of what's ahead and it falls my lot to tell them the future. They come to me with no future and I have to invent one for them.

"A little future that I pull out of myself here for each one of them." She must have pointed to some part of her body, her heart, liver, or head.

Scorpio began to feel like vomiting.

"Hollow children," said her mechanical voice in the dark, "hopeless sweet sixteens, emptier than the whirls of their waltzes, guys whose shoes have a greater destiny than they have themselves, women with a fraction of the future of their shopping bags . . ."

She seemed to have turned her back to him, speaking more and more to herself, to something inside herself or something that she was carrying.

"The cat," Scorpio recalled, "she lulls the cat with that lullaby."

His uneasiness grew as her words were transformed into purring. He had to get out and get some air. He left the place without being noticed.

He took the first pill or another one (he couldn't remember) when he got back to his apartment. He needed to enter a dream and, in case he was already dreaming, to sink still deeper into it.

"To sleep seven days in a row," he murmured in a thick voice.

The telephone awakened him, a voice from the institute asking if he were perhaps sick.

"I'll be by this afternoon," he promised, half asleep.

"It's night now," the voice protested. "Are you really all right?"

Scorpio pulled one leg out and then the other, sat on the side of the bed and looked at the face of the unwound clock. He said he was fine and would be in tomorrow.

The door of the balcony had been open while he was sleeping, and the rain had come inside the room. It was as if he'd made a long airplane trip, crossed countries with different time zones, and now found himself here.

How strange it was the way things had turned out for him now. The moon was a small disk, he heard the noise of neighboring televisions sets. To judge by the growth of his beard, a week had not gone by. He was thinking that she was still in the city. He felt hungry and thirsty and then had an urge to walk through the streets.

Changes were taking place in the institute. Furniture was piled up in the hallways and he mistook the entrance to his department.

"Now you're on the floor above," the new editor told him.

"But they can't put us so far apart," he responded to her in a roguish if somewhat mechanical tone.

On the floor above, the chief of research said, "Tell me you're all right now."

"I'm all right now," he said obediently.

"I'd like to tell you, then, that we're able to start some new investigations." The chief tilted his chair and leaned perilously backward. He seemed to be saying: "Watch out for the leap I could take now."

Scorpio thought about it for a moment.

At last he said, "I'd like to investigate what people turn to in order to keep on living."

Of the puzzled looks that followed, his own was as astonished as his boss's. Both were asking themselves where that came from. He decided to repeat it and then it sounded familiar and reasonable.

"What a topic!" he might shout in his boss's face.

The chief remained silent, pushing still farther back, and now seemed to be saying, "Look at me in this dentist's chair. I'm suffering."

And Scorpio recognized his negative reaction by that intensely concentrated expression. The chief began to talk to him about sociology, about any other discipline but history. He tried to evict the subject from the premises, sweep it from its niche in the institute.

"If not exactly involved in it," the chief advised him, " at least it verges on the field of philosophy, and this is a conversation between two working historians, right?"

Scorpio admitted to himself that he must have been in a very bad state to repeat the words of a dream to his boss. He stopped listening to the other's words, and when he began to pay attention again, his boss was recommending that he take some vacation time, saying he was authorizing it.

"It doesn't interest me now," Scorpio answered. "I have nowhere to go."

The chief made a slight gesture of discouragement: "It's true, every day it get's harder to get out of Havana." But he immediately began to soften his negative statement by switching to talk about movies, detective stories, and the new editor to go out with.

"One of these days he'll crack his head because of that chair," Scorpio felt sure. What meaning could there be in directing a department of history when history itself had no meaning for him?

He carried himself as if on vacation. This time he went up in the elevator and looked for the sign on the door. The door, however, seemed to have vanished the same way as had various events of that night. Where there'd been a sword, a flower, or some lips, nothing remained. What part of that night had he dreamed and what part was real? Instead of a bell he found a hole and stuck his finger in until he got a shock. Then he knocked on the door, and the door of a neighboring apartment opened.

"Veranda left, she no longer gives consultations," the half-seen neighbor informed him before closing the door.

Veranda . . . . He made as if to leave but returned to place his ear against the wood. He couldn't hear anything from inside but felt a presence, something pressed up against the other side of the door too.

To sharpen his hearing he closed his eyes. In the darkness of his squeezed eyelids two points of light appeared. They seemed to be approaching, to be coming from a long way off. As they came closer they grew larger, becoming two spheres of honey. Just before they started to drip, the spheres opened and he opened his eyes, startled: the eyes of the cat. The cat was there, on the other side.

He didn't wait for the elevator but took the stairs. The noonday light scorched the leaves on the trees and perhaps it would rain in the afternoon. He would have to spend two weeks without going to the institute; she would finally leave on Saturday. The cat truly existed, the astrologer was named Veranda and wasn't there. He remembered there were still some pills in the bottle. He would sleep with the door to the balcony closed and to hell with the rain or anything else.

Now that he found himself on vacation he would have liked to return to that city with a view of the bay from a hotel garden. And although it was the same area he was walking through now, he couldn't identify it. Where was he going to spend those two weeks?

He remembered a conversation with the former editor at the institute, dead now or retired. It was from her that he'd first heard of a place where one could spend one's working hours quite pleasantly.

"Like a bit of vacation tucked into the middle of a work day," she'd said.

The day clinic where he ended up was in an old mansion. The living room still served as a place to talk, one of the bedrooms was for doing handicrafts, and the patio was now used for sports. The medical treatments were not too tiring and every so often the sick residents would go out to buy their own cigarettes. Among the patients you could find real authorities on such matters as hypnotics, antidepressants, and stimulants. They called the drugs by pet names, names that lent them a constant intimacy.

One person in particular would say "La Trifu" to refer to trifluoperazine, as if speaking of a great soprano, a diva, and his conversations about drugs resembled opera plots. They discussed dosages for hours on end. The doctors came and went through the rooms and were never called to give an opinion. It was understood that their knowledge was only theoretical. Not a single one of those white coats had been put to sleep with those drugs. Some patients spent years going from one clinic to another, had seen case after case pass through. Scorpio asked one of those if anyone was ever cured.

"Of course. What did you think? This is not the sanitarium of *The Magic Mountain*."

There were few women. Or rather, few women worth noticing. One of them persisted in telling her dreams every morning. Almost everyone avoided her, especially another woman who cut her off sharply, warning "I don't like dreams."

That warning was the only thing ever heard from her. Unlike the others she kept silent. Scorpio called her Mystery. One day he heard she was dying of cancer.

He spoke of emotional loneliness in one group therapy session, in another he complained about having lost interest in his work.

"Professional anemia," one of the best-educated patients called it.

That's how the two weeks passed. At the end of his vacation he went to the institute one morning, notified his chief that he was in the middle of a period of treatment in a clinic and couldn't leave it now. He experienced the wariness of most people when faced with an infectious disease and discovered that, after all, it wasn't so different from the way he usually acted with others.

The next day he returned to the clinic in a cheerful mood. He was convinced that the causes of his stay there were eminently professional.

He played the covert historian. He never ceased to be amazed that each and every patient returned on his own two feet every morning. He noted the tears, the contention, the loquacity, the silence and the shouting as if they were all facets of the same abiding permanence.

"Look how we are holding on," the crew of patients seemed to be saying to him.

It was clear they had little to lose, but they would stay until they saw that little lost.

Each patient was converted into one of his historian's notes. The woman who would recount her dreams to no one presented her bare arms to him, as if her old and recent scars were smuggled wristwatches.

He met a prematurely aged man who blamed his condition on the blackouts.

"We live by halves," he said. "They black out one district so another can exist. When there's no electric light in the darkened house, I've had the security of knowing that another someone like me, another me in some illuminated part of this same city does things for me, lives my life.

"I don't know him, but he must also suspect, when his house is dark, that someone like me fills his time.

"We must meet each other without fail, come to some agreement. It's a matter of establishing something larger," he continued, "something that goes beyond the fate of only two individuals."

He called it The Lodge of Parallel Lives, an institution that would assign each one his double, and with the double, a complete life.

"He mentioned it to me too," said the teller of dreams.

She and Scorpio were side by side, weaving hats of palm leaves.

"It must be something like a lonely hearts club," the woman added, musing to herself.

Scorpio was thinking that perhaps the true language of wisdom was that of the tongue slowed down by means of chemicals, the language spoken by the man grown old before his time.

He tried to get close to him more often but the man issued warnings, saw enemies of his ideas everywhere.

"Maybe he's just crazy," said Scorpio, disheartened, and stopped bothering him.

Some days passed, the aged man stopped coming, and it was later discovered that he wasn't living at home either. The neighbors knew nothing about him.

"He found the other I he talked about so much," was the opinion of some.

Scorpio, however, only saw the house abandoned by the man and remembered another empty house, that of the astrologer, where he believed he'd heard a cat talk.

"Another one who leaves everything behind. He doesn't die, doesn't kill himself, ignores his belongings, is reduced to wandering."

"Skitalietz," he said, that's what the disinherited wanderers were called in Russian.

So many notices of missing persons, and he'd paid no attention to them. Outside, away from the mansion now turned day clinic, the city was full of skitalietzes, people who were apparently wandering aimlessly. His days in the clinic were coming to an end.

The certainty that he wouldn't be there the next morning lent him unusual agility. He moved on the basketball court as never before.

The outcome of the game came to rest in his hands. He dribbled the ball through the arched legs of an opponent and leapt in triumph toward the hoop.

With him leapt another body. The two found themselves in the air and Scorpio discovered the woman he had named Mystery. To keep her below him, he jumped higher, jabbed his fingertips into the air around the ball. Squinting against the sun he found then a distant image, that of a painting in which a man and a woman were floating above all the others. He wanted to float like that for a while, to fly over the city and watch all the movements of the inhabitants — perhaps that way, he'd find a meaning.

In a final effort of agility he opened his eyes almost at the rim of the hoop, and with surprise found those of Mystery also. His arm had only to make a smooth movement of renunciation to end this persecution. Something, however, held him back.

Scorpio had discovered in the woman's pupils two little lights, and he entered the darkness of the tunnel that had to be crossed to reach them. From far away he felt one of his arms drop the ball into the basket; then he traveled through an endless tunnel until he reached the ground where he fell into the arms of his teammates, who began to celebrate the game they'd won.

"What am I doing among crazy people?" he asked himself as they were slapping him on the back.

When they let him go, Mystery, that is, Veranda or whatever the astrologer was called, had left.

He thought about looking for her at her apartment but immediately gave it up. Who was she, after all? The few times he'd heard her speak in therapy he'd understood she wrote soap operas for the radio. Although she was without any doubt an astrologer, perhaps there wasn't much difference between a horoscope and a radio episode.

The telephone rang. The new editor of the institute wanted to know about his health, she was apprehensive about any changes.

"Changes, what changes?"

He remembered furniture piled in the hallways, the new location of his department. Well, now it was a matter of human changes.

"People outside the institute," she said. "Without work."

There was a silence on both ends of the line. He asked her if that was going to happen to her.

"People cling to their seniority rights," the editor explained.

"There's not another editor in the entire institute," he responded.

She said there'd be no more books.

He began to ask himself why he had to be the one to give her hope. This conversation made no sense. Sorrowful, in a thin voice, she told him then that he'd been let go, that they'd made one of those changes with him.

Scorpio said good-bye as well as he could, muttered something confused about remaining friends. Then he took one more pill than he should have and curled into a ball. A ball that twitched in the bed from time to time.

The following morning he did not find the chief in the dentist chair and missed him for the first time. They offered him the chance to go live in an agricultural camp and do farm work for a year.

"A camp in the country," he said to himself, "wouldn't be very different from a day clinic. More sweat, fewer pills. More confidence in the therapeutic virtues of work."

Otherwise, he would receive part of his salary for several months, enough until he found another job.

"I'm only a historian," he told them, "I don't know how to do anything else. What job am I going to find?"

At that moment he regretted not being trained for a broader type of work. He longed to be a carpenter, a mechanic, a brick mason. And again he considered the possibility of an agricultural camp — to plant, use his hands, earn his food by dint of backaches, observe the rains the same way the ancients observed them, put himself in tune with the cosmos, be in harmony, go back to the land. The land was wide enough for everybody! There would be land everywhere!

But now he could not leave the city. There was the possibility that wherever she was, things might not be going well for her and she might decide to return. In that case he was sure she would search for him. So he could not spend an entire year away from Havana. Every month he would collect the small salary they would be giving him and perhaps some way of earning money would turn up.

As he left the institute he missed his work for the first time. The old protests, the bad mood at getting up every morning, the slowness of the clock to strike five, the tedium of meetings, all such feelings were erased. Those years of work could now be summed up in articles published in the institute journal and in a couple of books stored in the institute library.

"They'll also close the library," he said to himself.

His fate was to lose things in order to understand later how much he loved them. Her, his job — what more would he have to lose in the times ahead?

"Keep going, keep going," he repeated to his legs. It weighed on him to leave the old building. His eyelids felt heavy, so he entered the first movie theater he came to and settled down to sleep through many continuous film showings until it closed.

He dreamed he was a seat in a movie theater and that it

wasn't so bad being a seat, after all. The darkness made his skin resemble velvet, the temperature was always ideal, and the scenery changed each week. What more could you ask for? A broom banging against his shoes woke him up. A thread of saliva descended from his lower lip to his shirt. He'd been there so long that spiders could have woven a web around him.

The woman with the broom glared at him the same way she looked at drunks. Without a movie the theater smelled of damp rugs and stale clothing. Outside it was night. He walked a few meters and was caught by the blackout in that part of the city.

"They've turned off the lights, so the movie should begin now."

He walked through a war movie. No alarms could be heard, nobody expected enemy attacks. Everything seemed to have happened already, all devastations. In the darkness the corners revealed their eroded profiles. Where earlier a building had stood they'd made a garbage dump and the moon glinted on the broken bottles. He said to himself that at least for once he had not made the wrong decision: apart from the institute, apart from her life, he still had the city, the ruins he was traversing. They were his shelter, he could not leave them.

He felt hungry, put a fried egg on the plate, and burst into tears. The flowers on the plate, the last survivor of a set of dishes, made him cry. He should do something, climb, swim, until he could extricate himself from that hole.

"From now on," he announced aloud, "there's nothing more from here on out."

And he remembered Mystery, Veranda, the astrologer soap-opera writer, the woman who floated.

"What may I call you?" he asked her. Because if she persisted in calling him Scorpio, he also wanted to call her by her sign.

He had surprised her just as she was leaving her house, her hand still on the doorknob.

"Call me Veranda," she was about to tell him, when he again asked her for her sign.

"Cancer."

"Cancer," he repeated. "Are you truly ill?"

"Truly ill. That might be one way of explaining it."

Scorpio remembered the night they had met for the first time. In the darkness she seemed to speak to him of something inside her. Perhaps she was reproaching the growing thing bent on killing her.

"You want to ask me if I will die from this 'truly ill.'"

He didn't dare answer. But she answered.

"Call me Veranda."

"Quite an odd name," he tried to tease her, to put the conversation on a less somber note.

"It's in the dictionary."

"It's the name of a place from which one looks out, right?"

"That's what I've done for many years."

The door remained half closed; he felt certain the cat was not there.

"Why didn't you tell me anything? You saw nothing?"

Veranda closed the apartment and looked into his eyes.

"I see nothing of the future. Only the past."

"And the present?" he asked.

She began to laugh.

"Who needs someone to tell them what's happening to them now?"

He should have said "I do" but he asked her about his past.

"You're a historian," she pointed out with a bit of irony. "Don't you know the past?"

"I'm asking you for mine," he demanded in a childish voice.

"It costs a lot of effort to extract from the rubble what you already know about yourself."

He raised his voice. What good was her gift of prophecy?

And suddenly she was in agreement with him, nodding fiercely:

"Of course, what good is it if I die in a short time?"

Scorpio was afraid to be alone with her.

"Have you never read it?" she asked now on the verge of tears. "Has nobody told you? Don't you sense yet that neither the future nor the past exists? That the present is the only thing we have?"

He felt hollow. Days and nights to form this empty space he'd become. And around the empty space, rage erupted like lava.

"And you waste the little time remaining to you in that clinic of crazies?" he shouted at the woman while shaking her.

Too surprised, Veranda offered no resistance. Scorpio too was suddenly astonished at the turn things had taken and removed his hands from her. He began to stammer what could be an excuse but was actually a desire: to take a train he'd never traveled on before, leave Havana, get off at some stop, preferably a small station.

"Something will have to happen then," he ended.

"To arrive in a country," she told him, "where there's not even one person you know by sight. With no money, not understanding a word of the language, and to become invisible there."

Was it a desire or a memory of hers? Scorpio felt in her words the conviction that comes only from what's already happened. Neither of them was clear about the intentions behind what they'd said. They went down the stairs. They had in common the desire to travel, yet they made it impossible for themselves to leave the city.

"There's something I lost here in Havana," he explained, "and I have to find it precisely here."

"My cat," she said, "I must rescue him. I think of how hungry he must be, the poor thing."

She tried to stay in familiar places, she was besieged at times by the presentiment that it would be easier to meet death if she went out a little ways into the countryside.

The two descended, fearful the stairs would end, end in the street, in the present. And, suddenly on the last four or five steps, they made a decision: at the exit of the building they would find themselves in the little railroad station, in a strange country. If there was only the moment, no other solution remained except to begin continually, to believe that each step was the first step.

And putting their legs into the sunshine of the street, then their torsos and their heads little by little, they appeared for the first time alive, one beside the other. They filled their lungs with air, stopped before one of the trees along the avenue not knowing it was a laurel or what it might have in common with the other laurels in the row.

Each tree was the tree. To walk one street became an eternity for them. Only after a long period of observation did they understand that the wall was the summary of numerous stones. They were unable to generalize, it was impossible for them to treat things by groups. They focused so intensely on people that they were mistaken for lunatics.

They came to the end of the avenue, to the Malecón, to the sea. Veranda asked him to help her onto the wall. Standing before the immensity, they could not keep up with all that was happening. They watched one wave until its end, but lost many others. If future and past did not exist, such immensity could not fit into the present. A single moment could not shelter it all.

At the end of the line of the Malecón, Scorpio spotted the hotel garden where the wedding celebration had taken place. That night he'd wished to live in the Havana seen from that spot. On leaving the apartment building he and Veranda had proposed something similar. He felt tired or sleepy. The darkness of closed eyes was not in future, present, or past, it was in no time. He opened his eyes to see what she was doing: she was still absorbed by the sea. The salt air blew in their faces and he let himself go as if he were the sail of a ship.

She moved a leg and Scorpio awoke.

"The blackout is back," Veranda announced.

To her it seemed like the return of the same electrical shut-off. It had become as natural and cyclical to her as day and night. Scorpio lifted a cramped arm, shook it as if to hurl it toward the water. She began to rub where his sleeping head had rested earlier.

"Aren't you hungry?" she asked.

"Yes." He began to lick the salt from his lips. Had she slept?

"Not at all."

She curled up on the wall.

"I have some food at home," she said, "but the darkness there does me in."

They walked toward his apartment. They ate and then

the blackout came. Veranda began to laugh: this time they'd gained a little on the dark. Later she became sad and said she was leaving.

"The light hasn't reached your house yet," he reminded her.

"I don't see much fun spending the night like this," Veranda replied.

"Take this key."

He searched in the darkness of the apartment for the same key that had been returned to him some weeks earlier.

"Give it to me some other night," she said.

Left alone he lay down on the sofa, positioning his back so that a spring sticking out wouldn't bother him.

No greater silence existed than the silences of those nights without electricity. Televisions and radios fell mute, refrigerator motors no longer snored, the buzz of insects in the dark city lost.

He turned on a tap to hear the water falling, he would squander his ration simply to have that music.

"We're left without light, without water," he said to himself, "even our pets are leaving us."

In the other room the tap cleared its throat, growled a few times before going dry.

"Perhaps we're dead without knowing it," he muttered.

Any effort to transcend the condition in which they found themselves would lead nowhere; from death there was no escape. He remembered a woman's arms covered with cuts. "I wanted to concentrate on understanding that point," he realized "that there is no way out."

"How bad we are at being dead!" he concluded as he closed the door of his house.

To make oneself invisible it wasn't necessary to set foot in another country; making his way through the blackout he was the invisible man. People sitting at the doors of their houses didn't see him go by. They didn't look toward the outside or the inside. There was no expression in their glances.

A man and his wife had brought chairs into the street. No cars passed. The man began to say something to his wife and she interrupted him:

"Over and over the same story," she murmured. He had come to that, her hero of old now only daring to bring his chair out to the street.

"Women," thought Scorpio. "They sweeten our ears with epic proposals, sing us to sleep with them. Later, they remind us of them as promises that came from us ourselves."

Lighted areas would announce themselves to the ear; he stalked like an ancient nocturnal hunter. A distant sound must be the murmur of someone calling. Later, more clearly, all the appliances going on at once would sound like a nearby river.

Scorpio listened to the murmur, the call, and uncertainty hit him suddenly. A hunter searched for food. What could be found along these streets? What difference could a little light make, after all? There, where it might be, a few hundred meters farther on, things would also be dead, a woman would cut off her husband's words in just the same way.

The city seen from the hotel and the one he had walked through with Veranda to the sea must now be in another part, it couldn't be this one. The same difference existed between them as between a nightmare and the telling of that nightmare the next day, when it would all seem harmless. What story was it that began with a wedding, followed by crossed telephone wires and a game of basketball? And that recently created commitment, ridiculous, with a woman he wasn't even attracted to, and on top of that would die soon? On waking up, there would be a moment when he would ask himself these and other questions, but now he couldn't pause.

"No universal questions."

His interest could not precede him by very much, nor could he travel toward the past. He took the precautions of travelers in strange territory.

"Don't wander far from this body that's walking," he told himself. "Past and future exist only as small attachments."

Farther off the impossible vistas began, the generalities capable of driving anybody crazy. He was on the verge of thinking that his life was too big for him, like an overcoat, that no matter how he stretched his arms, he could not find the cuffs. But the remains of some unconscious compassion kept him from such thoughts. A few steps away the light was shining; at the edge of it Scorpio discovered Veranda.

She remained in the dark. Her back was shaking, she was coughing or crying. Scorpio supposed she could have spent hours there. He came closer to the edge of her mystery and heard her singing or saying something in a very low voice.

When she turned around her eyes were moist. She looked at him for a moment as if he were an unknown passerby, then gave him a sad smile.

"Don't follow me any more," she said without an ounce of annoyance.

"It was by chance," he excused himself.

One more time. And every time she spoke to him she seemed to refer to a continuity established beforehand. Don't follow me any more. "Another night he'd give her the key to his apartment." It must be her discreet way of asking for future opportunities: she would go out of the dark toward the light other times, would find herself with him a few more nights. Why was she crying?

Two or three shadows of cats leapt from the garbage bin on the corner. Perched high on the heap, one remained turned toward them. It could have been there as long as she was, keeping watch in case of some possible attack. The cat moved, ruler of the hill of trash, and Scorpio managed to see the gleam of its pupils in the darkness.

He took a few steps toward the bin and the cat blinked. It

was a blink of security, marking the degree of closeness it would allow. Scorpio stopped. What rules of courtesy could exist between a man and a cat? The luminous eyes blinked again and, with utmost care, without losing the man from sight, the cat jumped from the bin, threw an oblique glance at the woman and followed his companions.

"What's his name?" Scorpio pressed Veranda.

He walked along the empty street, half light and half shadow. The cats went a few steps in front of him; he expected to catch up to them.

At his back, the woman gave an unintelligible shout that stopped him.

The cats were gone.

"What do people do in order to keep on living?" Scorpio shouted at one cat among the others.

His voice echoed in the plaza where he'd emerged and from the balconies the neighbors discovered the man who was shouting.

"What do they do to go on with life?"

"Call the police," people on one of the balconies demanded.

Scorpio stopped shouting and returned to Veranda. He made her sit down next to him in a doorway. Had she shouted the name of her cat?

"So you would let him go," she responded almost without a sound.

Scorpio opened her hands to find her face. He dried it

then with the handkerchief he was carrying.

"I did it for you," he said.

She took the handkerchief, spoke in a congested voice:

"We talk without coming to an agreement."

Her tears increased.

"He will not come back with me. He said that he doesn't want to see me die. That he wouldn't like being shut up with a corpse until somebody tore down the door."

"At least he doesn't know how to open doors," Scorpio said to himself.

Her words that referred to a corpse and death did not seem to touch her, she would not be the one dead.

"It's that he loves me too much to bear that," Veranda exploded at last.

Scorpio offered her his shoulder, took the key to his apartment from his pocket and put it between her fingers. She was crying so much the key fell to the ground and he had to put it in her hands again.

"Now, for sure, there's little left," Veranda admitted bluntly.

She held the key up as if he had placed a flower in her hands.

"I want to ask you something, Scorpio . . . . If you and I are alone when I die . . . ."

His face must have shown astonishment.

"It may seem sudden to you, but no matter. You will only have to remember it then. Before that, you can forget it . . ."

"I will act as if I didn't know," he agreed.

"Make sure that I am completely gone and leave the door open. Don't stay with me any longer then."

"I won't follow you any more," Scorpio promised.

A continuity existed for them that would end when Veranda's life ended. They were left with the time that she calculated would soon end, that and the space of a city. They were two passengers from different lands who happen to meet in a station and only have time for a cup of coffee. Was it worth the trouble to synchronize their watches? Veranda and Scorpio made their schedules coincide with pills.

They went counter to the blackouts, pooled the food they'd acquired, shared bread like two sweethearts in wartime, held each other's place in lines. They went to the movies to sleep, showed each other places they'd always found beautiful. He took her to a place where five streets began; she took him to a street in the form of a horseshoe. They went to a park with a Greek temple in the center, to a Chinese garden at the mouth of the Almendares River. One afternoon in a whitewashed patio they were in Ibiza, one dawn surprised them on an iron bridge, sure that in Bruges the boats moved just the same way.

He went with Veranda to the neighborhood of her childhood, and later showed her the one where he would have wished to be born if he'd been born in Havana.

Sometimes they waited out the blackout, and the darkness allowed them to speak of their pasts without shame. Then they were a pair of separate voices, the same as on the telephone at the beginning.

They discovered an old mutual acquaintance, and without knowing where he could be now, began to construct his detailed biography. He had not been especially important to either one of them, but they focused on him in meticulous fashion and tried to reconstruct his comings and goings. They wanted to know at what moments they might have met, years ago. It seemed to them a mystery that things did not happen simply because of some small detail.

It turned out to be difficult to separate coincidence and fatalism. Without fear they used reasons similar to those of any housewife: "Everything was already written in the book of life, and everybody has his hours there."

One evening Scorpio found her face had a lovely air, but the evening passed and he again lost interest in her possible beauty.

They saw groups of people leaving for the countryside, saw groups returning. Veranda noticed in those who returned the same rough appearance that she and Scorpio had. Among a crowd of people, he found his old boss and the new editor of the institute.

They spent afternoons in the shade of the Indian almond trees near the port. The red and green shade made them wish for the autumn that would never come. They were beneath the sprays of yellow flowers of some trees in Central Park.

"They are rhododendrons," he invented for her.

They followed the route of the street sweepers and adopted their familiar habit of reading whatever paper they found and gathering up pages torn from books. The collected piles of papers they called the magazine of the street. On certain nights of intense heat they slept beside some passengers at the closed doors of the bus terminal. They listened to the speeches of lunatics and gave them the few coins they carried, knew they were closer to them than to the others. They saw their tatters and sensed that in the long run they would walk around dressed the same way. They could no longer be historian and astrologer, they were now vagabonds. Their professions had turned them into tatters.

"Anyone can become like us," a vagabond confessed to them. "The recipe is forget to go back home."

They realized then they had lost the habit of returning to their houses.

"It can begin one evening, at the end of the workday, when one regrets having to go home," the vagabond explained. "If it coincides with a morning when one may have regretted having to work, the bomb has a fuse."

"Some people go to bed and the moment they begin to review the day and to endure the thought that this day will be followed by another, they would love to find the courage to leave it all."

"But one needs courage to get up," Scorpio thought. "To go to work, go back home, rest a little on the weekend, start over on Monday . . . . What people call a normal life."

Veranda was listening to them with a meditative air. On nights when it was impossible for her to sleep, she longed for that life.

"It doesn't matter what one decides to do," she said, "whatever it is will become as difficult as possible."

On occasions their conversations seemed to take place beside a fire, on a beach at the end of the world. It was getting hard to be alive. But better alive than dead.

The priest of a little church took them for brother and sister, a ferryboat pilot who steered toward Casablanca at dawn, for husband and wife, and the rest thought they were mad. They approached someone to ask directions and before they could say a word were given money.

A girl wanted to interview them. They met in a park, watching a brigade of workers who were sawing the most dangerous limbs from some trees. What they said to her would never come out in newspapers or television or radio.

"Perhaps you're not a journalist?"

"More or less," she responded in a very sweet voice.

"What exactly is more or less?" Veranda asked.

"Social worker."

"And that's a profession?"

Veranda's question was the first step in a dialogue of comedians. They assumed the manner of comic artists.

"So all workers are not social workers?" Scorpio pointed toward the men sawing limbs.

The girl noticed the men at work.

"The rains are coming," she predicted. She sweetened her voice in a particular way for certain questions: "Do you have a place to sleep? What do you eat? You're not experiencing pain?"

Scorpio scrutinized her. She'd be ten years younger than he was and took the liberty of treating him the same way she'd treat a homeless old man.

Veranda cut her interview short:

"Don't waste your time this way, girl. There are too many questions and we can't answer them. What you need is a single question that sums them all up. A very general question, all encompassing . . . ."

Veranda turned her eyes to Scorpio. Now it was his turn. Scorpio then put his question to the girl and left her looking as if she'd heard it from the mouth of the cat.

"It's a philosophical question, you know. We are two park philosophers. He specializes in observing the behavior of those social workers over there. In this piece of paper I picked up I study the figures for honey production in the provinces."

They treated the social worker as if she were the one in need of care. That tone aroused the girl, erased all her sweetness in one stroke.

"It would be better if we'd hit you, right?" Scorpio's words sounded harsh. "Then we'd be a simpler case."

He took Veranda's arm and they hurried away.

Her apartment was closer than his, and after a long time they went back.

Scorpio didn't know what accounted for Veranda's unease. From the bathroom, while he was shaving his beard of so many days, he heard her stumbling in the kitchen. She was opening and closing doors to find things that fell from her hands. He supposed she had lost the habit of domestic gestures, just as he no longer had his old skill in shaving.

"For a long time they prohibited my consultations," she recalled for him. "Astrology, divination, were illegal things. I never stopped doing it, so I know very well what it means when one of those characters arrives — a social worker, an inspector or the plainclothes police."

Scorpio couldn't take the meeting in the park as more than an accident that he regarded as of no great importance.

"You must have put columns of numbers in some book of yours," she said.

"Statistics," he admitted with astonishment.

"Did you or didn't you?"

"They are in there, yes. What does it matter now?"

"Very simple. Everything has to be in numbers. The

quantity of honey by province . . ."

Scorpio could live in the street, stop shaving, but he knew that the moment his ideas began to wander he would be on the road toward stupidity or madness.

"Why are you talking to me now about that honey?" he almost shouted.

"Not honey! I'm talking about us, about what's going to happen to us. We're a pair of numbers in a column. You can escape from your work and your house, get out of your duties, but you cannot stop being a number."

Veranda was speaking from her three-legged stool and her reasoning now stunned Scorpio.

"They'll pursue us until they have us in the proper column."

"There must be a population of vagabonds," he interrupted her. "Missing or abandoned, I don't know what they're called. A statistical population."

"That's right. The same as what happens with animals in danger of extinction. They make some sort of mark on you, they put a ring on you to keep track of where you are, to learn where you go. They take a census of the few who remain in order to . . ."

The blackout cut her words short. They were very near the wall that closed the dead-end alley, and an alley like this, they knew, was the ultimate trap for any vagabond.

"It may be there's no other way to make history," he seemed to apprehend in the darkness.

She said "Well," or something of the sort.

They took their pills, said good-night to each other. Scorpio spent hours sitting on the sofa where he would sleep. He stroked his clean face that seemed to belong to a brother he hadn't seen for a long time. Veranda's cough in the next room kept him awake. Later he slept a little and Veranda again awoke him with her attack of coughing.

He found she was out of bed.

"Veranda?"

"Change in the weather," she explained.

At noon Scorpio saw the rain coming straight down, without wind. From the sofa he figured that this day would be followed by many others when it would inevitably rain. Havana, drowned enough by blackouts, would also be made narrower by the rain. It would become more like a mere quarter, less easy to move through.

He walked for a while. The buildings without their paint, seen through the rain, took on their true nature. They were embellished by what little shading the rain lent them.

He looked at the sky, the two rows of houses, the drops that were falling without slanting: it was the same as a set constructed for a movie. A wet day accentuated the fictional quality of everything.

He leaned over a puddle. In the water of the puddle a face vibrated, too thin, unknown. Scorpio felt himself to be the neediest of men, there beneath the rain. He was about to burst into tears at the very moment that a police car stopped next to him. They politely made him get into the car.

Little good it had done him to shave; the social worker in the back seat had recognized him.

"And the woman?" she inquired.

Certainly she was still sleeping.

"Who?"

The girl whispered to one of the policemen and the car began to move slowly. They were searching for Veranda nearby.

"What have I done?" he asked in a ridiculous voice.

"Nothing," the girl and the policeman told him in chorus.

"You're going to be all right," she continued. "You won't get wet any more."

He was an animal they were saving from drowning.

"They'll just put a mark on me," he consoled himself, "turn me loose on dry ground."

He moved an arm in search of the pills and the man beside him became a bit alarmed.

"He's not dangerous," the social worker said as if speaking of the rain.

She no longer had the sweet voice.

They were going to intern him for a few days in a home for ambulants.

"So that was the word," he said to himself. "Ambulants."

They asked that he empty all his pockets and searched among his belongings for some documentation. While nothing among those objects referred to a past, the bottle of pills could give them an indication of how much of that past had been erased. They took the bottle and sent it to a doctor.

He gave them his name. Not Scorpio. Occupation skitalietz.

"It's Russian." He spelled it out.

They asked if he was Russian.

"They want a nut," he predicted. "They want to make a nut out of me."

It took him some time to explain what being a skitalietz consists of. The officials were very surprised to learn that he had a house to live in, a house all to himself. They took rapid note of the address; they must have thought it was a lie.

Here they could assign him only a small room. Everything would be tight after having had all of Havana.

He talked with a psychologist.

"One can get tired of being reasonable," he admitted. "It's not being crazy, and not a crime either. Tell me what I'm doing here."

The psychologist asked him to join him on a tour of the premises. They went out into the garden.

"This place is no stranger than a park or a street," he responded at last. "Tell me why if you had a house you were living in the street."

"If I answer him that I'm free he'll laugh in my face," Scorpio said to himself. "I'm not free, I'm here."

It had stopped raining and the leaves shone beneath the

gray sky. Scorpio came to the conclusion that nobody could be free if only one single *here* existed while so many infinite elsewheres were beckoning.

"I don't know what else to do with my life," he remarked. "I must have the heart of a skitalietz."

They were walking through the clear air. The interviewer was concentrating on his breathing exercises.

"The police who brought me said I was not accused of anything."

"Certainly not."

"And now you ask me what I was doing in the street. If I'm not accused, what do you want me to testify to?"

The psychologist placed the bottle of pills before his eyes. Did he have a prescription?

Scorpio said yes, and the consultation was over.

Ambulant was a tentative category. Passage through the ambulant home ended in detox centers, old people's homes, psychiatric hospitals, return to families. As for him, they'd dispatch him off to a madhouse, he was almost sure.

His first night was melancholy. The little window showed a tree in the distance, beside a road. At the moment of sleep he dreamed he'd spent the night huddled at the foot of the tree.

The pills changed color the next day and they didn't allow him to take them himself. A nurse waited patiently until he swallowed them and then opened his mouth to be sure. They transferred him to a psychiatrist, who rather than talking or asking questions, busied himself singing fragments of arias in a low voice. "Non posso disperar," Scorpio also sang, going from room to room.

They lent him some books, most of them he'd already read. They introduced him to someone who could be his partner for dominoes. At a game table he once again met an acquaintance from the day clinic.

"The Lodge of Parallel Lives," he whispered to the man in the middle of the game and only at the end of the match did his password have an effect.

The man, much more aged, took him aside. He spoke hurriedly under his breath. He wanted Scorpio to forget the old proposal, not associate it with him anymore. He no longer wanted to take part in any plot, but only to live peacefully. He declared that everything he had proposed before existed now in dominoes, and he just hadn't realized it.

He wasn't clever, he was blind. He spoke of revelation or re-education, it wasn't clear to Scorpio. He could find in his domino partner what he had searched for before in a double. Together the two of them could move something forward and at the end, in winning the game, the sensation of a more complete life would be reached for both.

"But it's only a game," Scorpio protested.

What more did he want? Men cannot go any farther.

"Only one thing is missing," the man admitted sadly. "Alcohol. Don't you miss it?"

Scorpio missed Veranda. He returned again and again to his last image of her as she lay sleeping soundly after a bad night.

The days of rain went on. What would she do in this harsh time? Perhaps he'd never get to see her again, he would not be present at her death. That, at least, would be a relief. He wouldn't have to leave her corpse alone with the door open.

Night came and he thought of her even more. In one of his dreams Veranda had the face of someone who had gone far away.

Two or three weeks later (Scorpio couldn't be certain) they brought her to the home for ambulants. It was not she herself, but what remained of her. Outside it was raining. The social worker had ordered them to look for her.

The last drops of rain ran down Veranda's sunken cheeks, her breathing was labored, and she barely spoke. She seemed as if taken from a war documentary. Scorpio found her dirty, smelly; he embraced her and she cried. They were interned, but together.

He gave the personal data for the recent arrival and when they asked if she suffered from any illness, Scorpio looked into her eyes.

"Asthma," was the only thing Veranda said.

Her voice also seemed to belong to another.

Scorpio showed her the garden after the rain, sang for her the fragment of aria stolen from the psychiatrist, took her as partner in his domino game. He wanted to open for her an impossible space of freedom. Veranda, on the other hand, paid attention to him merely for brief moments. She remained silent, concentrating only on her breathing, with eyes of a fish out of water. In the middle of a conversation or a game she seemed to be waiting for someone to whisper to her what she should say. Her eyes easily filled with tears and one evening she complained of pain in her side.

"Now for sure she's going to die," Scorpio thought, and behind her back reported her cancer.

He told them on a Saturday afternoon, and on Monday morning they would transfer her to a hospital. Neither of the two ate any lunch on Sunday. They went out to the garden together during the siesta. A fine rain began and they had to go into the game room.

Some flies buzzed against the door. Veranda stared at them, trapped between the metal screen and the rain. The entire day took on a tone of finality, of farewell. Very few words remained.

Veranda opened the door so the flies could come in. One of them lit on her hand and she showed it as if it were a jewel.

"What a miracle life is," she said without words.

He watched the behavior of the flies in the closed room.

"Freedom can consist of a closed space that's a little larger," he answered without parting his lips.

The two wept. Veranda embraced him and trembled like

a sparrow beneath a splash of water. He encircled the emaciated body, perceived the fragility of her bones and felt like breaking them one by one.

With his mouth he sought her dry mouth, the broken breath that still remained to her. Gestures they had never made were the only way of parting. Scorpio embraced in the woman a mound of dry leaves. He removed the first layer, scorched by the sun, and as he put them aside, found moist leaves, went along the path toward the rotten heart of things, to the dampness where flies, centipedes, worms wallowed.

He entered her fearing he'd awaken the animal eating her from within. The crab came through the dark corridors of the woman's body, poisoned its fluids, cut with its pincers the small amount of healthy tissue. Scorpio had to send his message of life inside and then retreat. He pushed, pressing deep inside against the hard rind of the cancer. He spurted at the same moment one of the pincers tried to decapitate him, breathed deeply the air of water.

She remained embracing him a long while, then let go, was still alive.

Neither of them slept that night. The tree on the side of road was doubled over before the wind. The night was so bad that he could not imagine himself being at the foot of the tree. It was best to think of nothing, keep the walls and the mind equally blank.

He wasn't there to say good-bye to her. Veranda had no

amulet, no personal belonging to leave him as present. She asked for a few minutes alone, rolled the sheet around her hand, and with one skillful blow, killed a fly.

She placed it on the night table and asked as a favor that they give it to him.

Scorpio was called to the psychiatrist's office. They were going to transfer him to the day clinic closest to his house. They found something in him that could still be salvaged, something that could be rescued, and the psychiatrist allowed himself to sing one of his favorites, the mad aria from *Lucia di Lammermoor*.

During the journey toward the clinic the sun was shining and Scorpio discovered Havana once again.

Because of the rains two or three buildings had collapsed. Some things would have to be reborn inside him.

Of the former patients none remained in the clinic. He walked through the rooms, went out to the patio, passed though the recreation area and remembered Veranda.

He opened his door, and the entire apartment jumped on him like a dog. Dust, bills to pay. No letter. The few pieces of furniture had become old and rickety. He lifted the telephone to hear no sound, looked at the moon. Everything seemed to repeat itself: the same odd moon, the woman who went away, his love for the city in ruins, his stay in the clinic.

"Only now the pills are blue."

He put off the visit to Veranda for another day, and weeks

passed. One afternoon, on the telephone, the voice from the hospital asked if he were family. He said yes. They asked him then to take her home. He sold a couple of books and bought her some flowers with part of the money. In the white tiled room Veranda had turned into the skeleton of a little bird, had grown smaller, lived on tranquillizers.

"You won't have to care for her for very long," the doctor advised him.

She took the flowers with one of her little claws and tried a smile. She asked if they had given him her fly.

"A fly?" he had difficulty understanding her.

She nodded with the flowers.

"Of course," he agreed without comprehending. "Should I have brought it to you?"

Veranda said no with the bouquet and tried again to sketch a smile. He asked her which of the apartments she wanted to go to. She left the flowers on her breast. An ambulance took them to her building. Inside the elevator Scorpio was afraid the blackout would overtake them.

"No, no, no," he prayed in a very low voice.

The door opened on the floor where it was supposed to. She was going to die in the best of all possible worlds.

The surprise was to open the apartment and find it empty, cleaned out by thieves. Veranda complained:

"It will be without furniture."

He looked at the intact lock. They hadn't left a thing. He

seated her against the wall and from there Veranda looked at her old space with great care. Crouching next to her, he begged her to go to his apartment, where she would be more comfortable.

Veranda whispered that he should leave her here. She wanted to say that she saw no reason for him to be burdened with this, but she didn't have the strength to explain so much.

It broke his heart to see her seated there on the floor of the empty house. They had slept on park benches, in arcades, against the closed door of a bus terminal, at bus stops, and now she would die without a proper bed.

He asked her to wait for him, raced down the stairs. He didn't have enough money to hire any transport and had to drag the bed through the streets. The wheels of his cart seemed useless to him, people stopped him to ask if the bed was for sale.

Two or three times he could see the money they offered him and cursed himself for not taking it. He wanted to die right there of a heart attack and let them lay him out in the street, on that same bed.

She had slipped down from the wall and made a frozen bow toward the floor. Scorpio found that she was dead. He put the bed in the center of the room, covered it with some yellowed sheets. He was going to lose sheets, bed, and cart. And he had lost her. He observed her a moment more, ly-

IN THE COLD OF THE MALECÓN

ing in the boat of her death. He left the apartment open.

He remembered what she had called him the afternoon they made love. "Cat," she had said. He got in line at a bus stop, he would go someplace. The bus followed the sea and entered the tunnel of the bay.

As they came out into the bright sun, Scorpio realized that, after a long time, he was leaving Havana. He pushed his way to the door and got off at the first stop.

At the bottom of a slope was the sea. A kind of sparse grass was growing in a few spots. The sound of the sea erased all noise from the highway. Opposite the shore most of the liquid residues of the city were emptied out. Sweat, saliva, blood, urine, semen, shit, all mixed there with the salt water. At that point Havana life ended. He had the feeling that someone was watching him, that he was part of a movie set during a shoot of exterior scenes. He didn't know how to confront God or the camera.

# ABOUT THE AUTHOR

Antonio José Ponte was born in 1964 in Matanzas, Cuba. In 1980 he moved to Havana, where he lives now. After completing studies at the University of Havana, he worked for five years as an engineer in remote areas of Eastern Cuba. After leaving this profession to become a screenwriter, he wrote filmscripts for two full-length fiction films and a documentary. Today, he dedicates himself entirely to literature.

Ponte has traveled in Spain, Mexico, Columbia, Ecuador, Germany, and the southern United States. He has published three books of widely acclaimed poetry, collections of essays, novels, and stories; his work has been translated and published in France and in Spain. He is now working on a novel and another collection of short stories.

# CITY LIGHTS PUBLICATIONS

Herron, Don. THE DASHIELL HAMMETT TOUR: A Guidebook
Higman, Perry, tr. LOVE POEMS FROM SPAIN AND SPANISH AMERICA
Hinojosa, Francisco. HECTIC ETHICS
Jaffe, Harold. EROS: ANTI-EROS
Jenkins, Edith. AGAINST A FIELD SINISTER
Katzenberger, Elaine, ed. FIRST WORLD, HA HA HA!: The Zapatista Challenge
Keenan, Larry. POSTCARDS FROM THE UNDERGROUND: Portraits of the Beat Generation
Kerouac, Jack. BOOK OF DREAMS
Kerouac, Jack. POMES ALL SIZES
Kerouac, Jack. SCATTERED POEMS
Kerouac, Jack. SCRIPTURE OF THE GOLDEN ETERNITY
Kirkland, Will. GYPSY CANTE: Deep Song of the Caves
Lacarrière, Jacques. THE GNOSTICS
La Duke, Betty. COMPAÑERAS
La Loca. ADVENTURES ON THE ISLE OF ADOLESCENCE
Lamantia, Philip. BED OF SPHINXES: SELECTED POEMS
Lamantia, Philip. MEADOWLARK WEST
Laughlin, James. SELECTED POEMS: 1935–1985
Laure. THE COLLECTED WRITINGS
Le Brun, Annie. SADE: On the Brink of the Abyss
Mackey, Nathaniel. SCHOOL OF UDHRA
Mackey, Nathaniel. WHATSAID SERIF
Martín Gaite, Carmen. THE BACK ROOM
Masereel, Frans. PASSIONATE JOURNEY
Mayakovsky, Vladimir. LISTEN! EARLY POEMS
Mehmedinovic, Semezdin. SARAJEVO BLUES
Minghelli, Marina. MEDUSA: The Fourth Kingdom
Morgan, William. BEAT GENERATION IN NEW YORK
Mrabet, Mohammed. THE BOY WHO SET THE FIRE
Mrabet, Mohammed. THE LEMON
Mrabet, Mohammed. LOVE WITH A FEW HAIRS
Mrabet, Mohammed. M'HASHISH
Murguía, A. & B. Paschke, eds. VOLCAN: Poems from Central America
Nadir, Shams. THE ASTROLABE OF THE SEA
O'Hara, Frank. LUNCH POEMS
Pacheco, José Emilio. CITY OF MEMORY AND OTHER POEMS
Parenti, Michael. AGAINST EMPIRE
Parenti, Michael. AMERICA BESIEGED
Parenti, Michael. BLACKSHIRTS & REDS
Parenti, Michael. DIRTY TRUTHS
Parenti, Michael. HISTORY AS MYSTERY
Pasolini, Pier Paolo. ROMAN POEMS
Pessoa, Fernando. ALWAYS ASTONISHED
Pessoa, Fernando. POEMS OF FERNANDO PESSOA
Peters, Nancy J., ed. WAR AFTER WAR
Poe, Edgar Allan. THE UNKNOWN POE
Ponte, Antonio José. IN THE COLD OF THE MALECÓN